## A psychotic madman unleashes an unstoppable nuclear hell

A searing flash of light burned its way into Track's eyes, and a low rumbling roar shook the Earth to the very center of its core.

"Krieger has won," was all Track could think about as his senses reeled from the tremendous force of the five-hundred-kiloton thermonuclear explosion.

Radiation burrowed into his pores and set his skin on fire.

He was a witness to the ultimate act of global terrorism, and he was powerless to stop it.

The world around him was ripping apart.

# TRACK
## Atrocity

# JERRY AHERN

A GOLD EAGLE BOOK FROM
# WORLDWIDE

TORONTO · NEW YORK · LONDON · PARIS
AMSTERDAM · STOCKHOLM · HAMBURG
ATHENS · MILAN · TOKYO · SYDNEY

For my nephew, Sgt. George Smith—
a hell of a good buddy all these years.
He paid me to say this!

First edition June 1984

ISBN 0-373-62002-0

# 1

"The coppers are on to us, Devlin," whispered a hoarse, urgent voice.

Devlin Martin glanced sideways at Jimmy O'Shea. O'Shea's poker-straight flame-red hair was in disarray, his bright blue eyes pinpoints of agitation.

"You're a good man, Jimmy," said Devlin with a grin, "but a Nervous Nelly. If the coppers are givin' us the eye, it's all the more reason we have for plantin' our little surprise package and goin' on with our business."

Martin lit a cigarette off the butt of the one that had been burning against his lips a second earlier and tossed the dying stub on the hard terrazzo floor of London's Heathrow Airport.

An old custodian, who looked like the brother of the broom he was pushing, stopped his sweeping and glared at Devlin Martin for an instant. Martin let his mouth spread wide in a grin and cocked his tweed cap a little more jauntily over his right eye. He shrugged his shoulders as he stabbed his hands into the pockets of his dark-green corduroy slacks and walked on. "But Devlin," protested O'Shea, "if they see us plant this thing—"

Martin's sharp look penetrated his shorter companion. O'Shea was clutching the briefcase containing the six sticks of dynamite against his chest like a mother protecting her child.

"We're almost to the locker banks now, Jimmy,"

said Martin. "We've got guns and likely the pansy-assed coppers don't. We've got the car waitin' for us outside. Tell me now, is it better that the coppers arrest us with a bomb in our possession?"

But Devlin Martin glanced over his right shoulder all the same. Fifty yards back down the corridor a man dressed in a worn suit and shiny black shoes studied a copy of the *Times*. Martin whispered the word "copper" under his breath and kept walking, half listening to the airport public-address system to try to pick up the security-code phrases that would alert him to the presence of Scotland Yard.

Twenty paces away stood the locker banks he had targeted, adjacent to the baggage-claim area. A lot of people would be around when the dynamite sticks blew.

O'Shea was talking again. "That one with the shiny shoes readin' the paper, Devlin, I tell you he's on to us."

"We're almost there, Jimmy—be easy, lad." Devlin Martin craned his neck, openly looking over his shoulder. The man with the shiny shoes hadn't followed them, but by the way he stood and held the newspaper, he could be watching them.

Devlin Martin stopped beside the lockers. He turned and deliberately stared at the man with the shiny shoes. "A copper—right you are, Jimmy," he said to O'Shea. "Now give me the bag if you don't mind."

The policeman, if he was one, looked across the baggage-claim section toward them.

"He'll see us. They'll find the dynamite," said a worried O'Shea.

"I've a way of fixin' that, Jimmy," said Devlin, as he put the battered leather briefcase inside the locker, closed it and pocketed the key. He slipped his right hand under his coat and withdrew a vintage 1917 Colt revolver in .45 Auto Rim, the barrel cut to three inches and a new front sight sweated on. He pointed the revolver, stomping his foot to steady himself as he leaned into the shot.

Martin double actioned the trigger once, and the boom of the .45 thundered in the box of concrete, steel and glass surrounding him. The inquisitive stare of Shiny Shoes dissolved as his forehead split apart.

A young woman standing nearby started to scream. Martin coolly raised the Colt and, aiming for the neck, shot her in the head.

"The new cartridges you made up shoot a bit high, Jimmy," was all he said as he pulled his hat low over his face and started to run.

As Martin rounded a corner past the baggage area he could hear O'Shea's feet pounding the floor beside him. He slowed and then stopped.

"Coppers!" he snarled. Two men in plainclothes, faces he knew as well as his own, were running toward him—Sir Edward Hall of Scotland Yard and Tompkins of the Home Office. Martin aimed the chunky Colt at Hall and fired two quick shots. Hall threw himself against a pillar, and a pistol appeared in his hand.

"The damn whistles now!" Devlin Martin shouted, hearing police whistles blowing from behind. Gunfire from Hall and Tompkins hammered toward him. Jimmy O'Shea cried out, and Martin turned. O'Shea's left hand was a bleeding stump and his face contorted in fear and agony.

Martin's only thought was that O'Shea could tell where the bomb was hidden.

"Lad," said Martin softly and he shot his friend twice in the face. As the red-haired man reeled back, Martin snatched up his compatriot's fallen Walther P-38. He fired the 9mm pistol twice at the approaching poice and started to run toward the Arrivals terminal.

DAN TRACK LOOKED AT HIS NEPHEW, George Beegh. "Why am I carrying my attaché case and my stuff bag when all you've got is a stuff bag? You're bigger and younger than I am. Here!" Track shoved the attaché case at the well-muscled dark-haired man beside him.

"Carry your own damn briefcase!" George snapped.

"Hell of a disrespectful way to talk to your uncle," Track teased.

"You try giving me that briefcase again, you'll see how damn disrespectful I can get!" George laughed, shoving him a little.

Track feigned left and slapped the attaché case against George's exposed midsection. George grabbed at it reflexively as Track let go and stepped away. People were looking at them, some of them had faces he recognized from the transatlantic flight from New York.

"I'm not gonna carry your lousy attaché case, Dan! I'm just gonna leave it here, so help me!" George shouted after him.

As Track started to turn and say something, he heard his name paged over the public-address system. A disembodied but distinctly feminine voice directed him to go to the nearest courtesy phone. There was a message.

To his far right, Track spotted one of the phones and started walking toward it. He glanced back at George who still held the attaché case as though he were going to drop it to the terminal floor. He couldn't read lips, but he could tell what George was muttering as he started after him.

Track picked up the telephone receiver.

An anonymous voice said, "Paging."

"I'm Daniel Track, you have a message for me?"

"One moment please, sir."

Track looked away. George was beside him, saying

under his breath, "I'm not carrying your damn briefcase."

"Yeah, but you're so much stronger than I am, and tall, really tall," pleaded Track.

"Bullshit!" exclaimed George. "How come I'm always stronger and taller whenever there's something to carry?"

The sound of a new connection drew Track's attention back to the phone. "Hello?" Track said.

"Hello, Dan? Chesterton here. Did you and young George have a satisfactory flight?"

"Yeah, just fine," Track replied with a nod.

"Dan, I know I was to have met you and George for dinner," continued Chesterton, "but I wondered if I might beg off and promise London's best breakfast instead. Something unexpected has come up here."

"Any problems?" Track asked.

There was a long pause, followed by the sound of Chesterton clearing his throat. "Just the opposite, really. You might recall the German air hostess I mentioned to you when we met in London some time ago. The one with the auburn hair. It was just before we found out that Krieger had stolen the hundred 500-kiloton thermonuclear warheads. Her name is Johanna Gruber."

"Yeah, I remember. She was all you could talk about that night over dinner."

"Quite. Well, I'd given her my telephone number and she called. We're, ah, having dinner here at my flat this evening. You and young George would be perfectly welcome, of course," Chesterton managed to add. "My man always cooks as though he were still feeding his regiment."

"You and Johanna Gruber, huh? Naw, breakfast will do just fine for George and me, if you're out of bed by then," Track added wryly.

"I really doubt that on a first date," said Chesterton,

but not without a note of hope in his voice. "Thank you for the vote of confidence at any rate. I'll ring you up at your hotel, then come around and collect you and George for that breakfast so we can chat."

"Don't do anything I wouldn't do," Track advised him as the line clicked dead. Track hung up.

He looked at George. "Well, dinner's off. Sir Abner's got himself a hot date, a German stewardess he met," he explained.

"Sure, a hot date just like Tassles LaToure I'll bet. Jesus, she was sixty-three years old," said George as he slammed Track's attaché case toward him.

"You never asked how old she was when you wanted a date with her," Track chided George. "You were only interested in the fact that Tassles used to be a stripper before she became my secretary."

"I'm still gonna get you for that, Uncle Dan, so help me."

Track laughed. "Come on, let's get our luggage and I'll buy you dinner and a drink."

"Bribing me won't help," cautioned George.

Track started toward the baggage-claim area, checking the overhead sign. He'd been hearing something odd for the last moment or so, and now he heard it again.

"Is that a gunshot?" he said aloud.

The sound came again. It *was* a gunshot. Then another and another.

The sounds were louder each time. At the far end of the corridor, Track saw a flurry of movement. A scream, shrill and piercing, sounded from there as well.

Track shoved his attaché case at George and started to run toward the sounds. There was more gunfire, a faint-sounding police whistle, a shout—he couldn't make out the words.

"Dan!" Track glanced once behind him. George, holding the attaché case, was running after him.

Ahead, Track saw a man running toward him. The man wore a hat pulled low over his face, a tweed jacket and dark slacks. Profiled for an instant as he turned, the mysterious figure revealed a revolver. "Aww, shit," Track muttered. The man was less than a hundred yards from him.

Behind the gunman, Track could see uniformed policemen with their truncheons brandished.

The man reloaded the revolver on the run as Track charged toward him. The tweed-capped figure saw him, and just as he started to raise the revolver, Track heard George shout, "Hey! Over here! Police!"

Abruptly, the fugitive stopped, his head snapping right. He was buying George for a half second, Track told himself. Track rushed toward the man, the stuff sack swinging on its strap as he slammed it toward the gunhand.

The revolver breathed fire, and the man holding it wheeled around as Track let go of the strap. Track pivoted, and his right leg snapped up and out. The revolver roared again as the bottom of Track's shoe kicked into the gunhand. The gun flew out of the man's hand and across the corridor as he dropped to his knees.

Track launched a kick toward the mean, sinister face, but, in a defensive move, Devlin Martin's hands flashed out. Something glittered as it fell from his left hand, making a metallic sound as it hit the floor. Martin grabbed at Track's right ankle and pulled.

Track fell back, his balance gone. He twisted his body as he started going down and caught himself on his outstretched hands. Track kicked with his left foot against his rival's head. He could feel the pressure release on his ankle, and he rolled onto his back.

"This tough nut wasn't about to give up now," Track thought as he saw the man scramble up and grab for the thing that had fallen from his hand. As he jumped to his feet, Track saw it. It was a key, a locker key.

The bastard was moving toward a ventilation grate at the foot of the wall off to his left.

"The key!" shouted Track, and he lunged forward. His victim threw himself against the grate like a cornered animal, and his hands splayed over it. The sound of metal clinking against metal reached Track's ears as he wrenched the clawing figure free of the wall, jerking him forward, off balance. Track's right came back and hammered forward, his knuckles exploding in pain as he unleashed an uppercut against rock-hard jaw.

His opponent's head snapped back, and his body went limp. Track let the pathetic-looking shape fall. He stared down at his right fist. Tiny lines of blood were etched across his knuckles where the skin had flecked away. In the background, he heard a police whistle and the pounding of heavily shod feet.

George was on his knees beside the unconscious body of Devlin Martin, peering through the grate. A blur of uniforms surrounded them both, and an authoritative voice informed them they were under arrest.

Over the shouts and commands of the uniformed police, the loud murmurings of the crowd, and George's vehement protestations, Track heard someone calling his name.

Sir Edward Hall, deputy superintendent of Scotland Yard, shouldered his way forward and shouted, "Release that man, the one with the blue suit and the thick mustache."

George wailed, "Hey, what about me?"

Track smiled at his nephew. "Do I know you?" he said.

"All right," responded George, "I'll carry the damn attaché case!"

"Who pays for dinner?" Track asked as the police started to drag George off.

"Okay, okay. I'll pay for dinner, too," George pleaded.

Track grinned, and as Sir Edward Hall came up beside him, he said, "Sir Edward, that tall man over there with the black hair and thin mustache is my nephew. Helped me stop this creep, whoever he is."

"Right." Hall turned away, calling to the uniformed officers, "That man as well. Release him immediately!"

Then Hall turned to Track. "He had a key," he said.

"A locker key," replied Track. "He shoved it down that grating before I could stop him."

Hall summoned a uniformed sergeant at the far side of the crowd. "Belton, remove that grating and search behind it immediately. Martin pushed the locker key through."

"Right, sir!" responded Belton.

Hall was bending over the motionless body, trying to stir him. "Out. Unconscious. Damn the bloody luck."

"Hit him too hard, I guess," Track interjected.

Hall turned to Track, his voice a whisper. "Sound reason to believe this one and one other man, both IRA, planted an explosive device of some sort in one of the lockers. Our men are already going through the locker bank, but there are hundreds of lockers there. The officer we had observing their movements was shot to death, and this one—" Hall gestured to the unconscious man "—this bastard shot his own mate, I'm afraid. Killed him instantly."

Track let out a long breath. "Why don't we help you with those lockers," he said.

"The device could explode at any moment. A bomb-disposal team is on the way," Hall said as he broke into a loping run.

Track called over his shoulder, "Hey, George!"
Then Track started to run as well.

THE ENTIRE BAGGGE-CLAIM AREA had been cordoned off.
Uniformed police, dark-coveralled SWAT team members—the London Metropolitan Flying Squad—and
plainclothes officers were tearing through luggage on
the floor before the lockers. A lead man moved from
locker to locker and opened each using a set of master
keys. The man with him inspected the inside, and if
there was a case shouted to one of the plainclothesmen.

"What can we do to help?" Track asked Hall. "Just
open suitcases?"

"But carefully, there's no telling how the bomb might
be disguised," replied Hall.

Track glanced at George. His nephew had already
dropped to his knees and begun sorting through a suitcase of clothing, and not very clean looking, either.

Track found a space between one of the ragged ranks
of overnight bags and dropped into a crouch. Taking a
case, he started to open it, slowly. His palms were
sweating.

It had been five minutes by the black-faced Rolex Sea
Dweller on his left wrist when someone shouted, "Hey,
we've got it!"

Track went to get up, the contents of a suitcase scattered in front of him. Half the clothes were women's
clothes, expensive-looking things, although a bit large.
He started to stuff the things back inside—slips, bras, a
pair of shoes in a plastic bag. There was something odd
about them.

He could hear one of the bomb-disposal experts
shouting, "Clear the area. This thing's about to blow.
There's less than a minute on the timer! Clear the
area!"

Track started to his feet then stopped abruptly. At the

bottom of the suitcase was another plastic bag. Inside it was a man's shoe.

He almost felt like a voyeur, exploring someone else's suitcase, especially one belonging to a—"A woman," he whispered, half aloud.

Hall was shouting something to him, but Track didn't look up. He took out the man's shoe. It was expensive, Italian.

Hall shouted again, "Dan—get out of here!"

Track swallowed hard. He held the man's shoe and the woman's shoe side by side. They were the same length, the same width. He threw them down, and plowed through the suitcase. A man's sweater and a man's turtleneck emerged, a pair of white crew socks, a pair of men's underpants. Finally, a pair of faded blue Levi's, unisex in appearance.

"Dan!" cried Hall.

Track looked toward the urgent face of the Scotland Yard man. He licked his lips.

"I've got it! The bloody bastards lost this one," the voice of the bomb-disposal expert sounded.

Track looked down from Hall. He found the suitcase handle and lifted the luggage tag. He read the name out loud. "Johanna Gruber—Johanna—Johannes—"

He looked back at Hall. "Johannes Krieger," he almost spat out the name. "The terrorist. He's disguised as a woman, and he's with Sir Abner Chesterton right now."

"My God—" Hall's jaw dropped.

Track started to run. "George," he shouted over his shoulder, "hurry!"

## 2

Sir Abner Chesterton smoothed his shirt under the waistband of his gray flannel slacks as he walked across the room. "Fitch," he called out to his manservant, "I'll answer the door myself."

"Very good, sir," the voice came back, its military tone unmistakable, and slightly irritating.

As he donned his jacket, Chesterton wondered about Fitch. Why had he ever entered domestic service and left the military? Fitch was a fine mess sergeant but, by all objective standards, a terrible butler. He ran down the three stairs that led from the living room to the small but exquisite hallway entrance. Mentally, he shrugged over Fitch—Fitch was a decent man and reliable, however lacking in some of the customary niceties.

Chesterton stopped at the doorway as the bell rang again. He caught his breath and glanced at himself in the gilt-framed hallway mirror behind the small Hepplewhite table. He straightened the midnight-blue ascot and the collar of his pale-blue shirt, the brass-buttoned blazer he left open as he reached for the doorknob. A woman had once told him he resembled the late actor David Niven. But that had been years ago. He tried not to think about his graying, thinning hair.

He opened the door to Johanna Gruber. She was very tall for a woman. The figure was pleasant, the face beautiful, he thought. The auburn hair was rich and full. As he stepped into the doorway to welcome her, he could smell her perfume. It was the perfume she had worn aboard that flight from Germany. It wasn't really that many days ago. But the world had changed. Johannes Krieger had stolen one hundred 500-kiloton thermonuclear warheads from a U.S. government shipment and would have exploded one of them in Chicago, had it not been for the efforts of Dan Track, George Beegh, and perhaps himself. But Krieger had gotten away.

Chesterton suddenly realized the woman was staring at him. "Is there anything wrong, Sir Abner? You did expect me?" The voice was warm, soft and inviting.

"Expect you. My dear, I have anticipated you since that wonderful telephone message." He touched his right hand to her left elbow, ushering her in. She wore a luxurious gray fur coat, the kind with the pelts sewn laterally rather than vertically, trimmed with black leather. She looked wonderful in it, he thought. As he helped her out of the coat he said, "May I, my dear?"

"Yes, thank you, Sir Abner," came the soft reply.

As she turned to face him and smiled, he noticed the whiteness of her even teeth, and the fullness of her lips. Her eyes were brilliant blue.

Chesterton stepped back from her, but only a half step. She wore a black dress, the hem falling just slightly below her knees. A single strand of rich white pearls caressed a long alabaster neck. Pearl earrings to match graced her ears. The black leather handbag she clutched perfectly matched her shoes, which were high heeled. Chesterton admired her for almost flaunting her height. She was taller than he, he realized as he turned back to face her after he had hung her coat in the entrance closet.

"You look lovely," he told her, almost compelled to say that.

"Thank you, Sir Abner. You flatter me." She smiled again.

Even the faintness of her German accent had something appealing about it, something very European that was hard to define. "Are we alone?" she asked, her left hand gently primping her hair.

"Except for old Fitch, my manservant," Chesterton responded, "and after dinner has been served, he'll be taking the night off. May I offer you a drink?"

"All right," she said, and still clutching her leather bag she walked with him up the three steps leading to the living room.

It was a spacious and well-designed apartment, Chesterton thought as he steered her toward the bar at the far side of the room. Perfect for an intimate dinner, and far more intimate than the place in the country with all those rooms and drafty halls.

"I wonder what you might like to drink, Fräulein Gruber," he asked.

"Johanna," she corrected. "Perhaps a glass of white wine, Sir Abner. Whatever you might choose for me."

"There's no need to use my title, my dear. Please, to you it is just Abner. And white wine it is. A Chablis, perhaps, or something more German—a Hock as they were once called. A Rheinhessen?"

"Rhine wine, I like that." She smiled. She opened her bag and held a package of Virginia Slims, her long, manicured nails painted a light-pink shade.

Chesterton snatched up the table lighter from the end of the bar. It was in the shape of an owl, and he flicked back the owl's head, and rolled the striking wheel under his right thumb. Johanna Gruber bent her head forward and inserted the tip of her cigarette into the blue-yellow flame. As she exhaled a cloud of gray smoke, she whispered, "Thank you...Abner." After a long moment, during which their eyes met and held, Chesterton found a bottle of Rhine and began to pour it into a glass.

As Chesterton poured himself a glass of wine, Fitch entered the room to announce that dinner was almost ready and that if there was nothing else, he would be leaving. Johanna smiled and said, "I'd rather we be alone, and I'd like to serve you dinner. After all, your Mr. Fitch has everything prepared, hasn't he." It was more a statement than a question.

They had moved to the couch, and Chesterton sat beside her not knowing what to say. Something about her was so totally different from other women he had met.

He looked away from her for an instant, trying to compose himself when his eye was attracted to the telephone. The receiver was off the hook.

"The phone," he said, "I must have forgotten to replace the receiver after I—"

He heard a sneeze from beside him, a tiny sneeze calculated to draw his attention.

Chesterton turned and looked at Johanna. She was smiling, picking up her handbag from the coffee table. Opening her handbag, she started to pick through it with her long fingers. "One of the difficulties of my profession," she said. "I move from place to place so frequently, I never seem to adjust to the climate."

"Perhaps I should turn up the heat a bit," responded Chesterton. "I'd imagine being an airline hostess does take its toll in the sniffs-and-sneezes department." He smiled, starting to rise.

Sir Abner felt himself freeze in midmotion. The gun in Johanna's right hand was a blue steel version of his own gun, a Walther PPK-S, only he'd left his at his office.

"Yes, being a flight attendant is difficult, but being a terrorist is even worse—Abner." The voice was a man's, Germanic, cultured, calculating.

"My God!" Chesterton exclaimed.

"Go ahead," the voice came back, "guess who I am."

"Johanna," stammered Chesterton, "Johannes Krieger!"

"I was afraid you were going to try to get into my pants before you found out." Krieger, still looking like the beautiful Johanna, laughed, insanely loud.

"Damn you!" Chesterton rasped. He threw himself at Krieger, clawing for the gun, but Krieger was quicker. As he sprang up from the couch, the pistol hammered against the right side of Chesterton's head.

Chesterton rolled to the floor, between the sofa and the coffee table.

He started to his feet, but the muzzle of the Walther was quickly between his eyes and he remained motionless, on his knees. He stared at Krieger's legs, where the hem of the skirt stopped and the nylon stockings began. He cursed himself for being an old fool.

"Sir Abner," taunted Krieger, "you'll forgive me if I'm a bit more formal? But you are going to die, and however rapidly or slowly death comes to you is entirely of your own making. I need to know all that you, this man Daniel Track and the younger man know, everything dealing with my theft of the 500-kiloton nuclear warheads—all of it." Then the voice changed to Johanna's again, and Chesterton was filled with revulsion. "Please, Abner," Krieger cooed.

CHESTERTON OPENED HIS EYES. The needle Krieger had jabbed into his neck left his vision blurred, and he felt vaguely hung over.

Krieger sat on a barstool. Chesterton realized he was on the floor. He tried to move, but his hands were tied behind him. His ankles—he could barely make them out as he looked toward his feet—were bound, as well. He tried to speak, but there was something covering his mouth. Adhesive tape, he guessed.

Beside Krieger, on the bar, was the gas-flamed chafing dish Fitch would have used to keep the poulet

Marengo hot. A tiny object was in Krieger's hand. Chesterton tried to focus on it.

"Having trouble, Abner?" Krieger spoke in Johanna's voice again, and then his own. "This is an ordinary kitchen skewer, Sir Abner. I'm heating several just like it in the flame beneath the chafing dish. The chicken smells delicious, by the way. My compliments to Fitch. We have no time for drug therapy to induce your truthfulness, and with some people certain drugs can indeed induce heart attack—and I don't wish you dead yet. I need the information you can provide far too greatly to risk your demise."

Krieger smiled—Johanna's smile.

Chesterton felt vomit rising in his throat.

"Before I begin with the red-hot skewers," Krieger continued, "the testicles perhaps, or the inner ear, and soon the eyeballs themselves. But before this, Sir Abner, a word of advice. If the Hindus are right, and we return to this life again, and should you come back as a man instead of an ass, I might suggest that you ask a woman out only after you've first seen her in the nude."

Krieger laughed, but it was Johanna's higher-pitched laugh. Krieger rose from the barstool with what Chesterton interpreted as a calculated taunt, smoothing his hands along his thighs. Krieger picked up one of the skewers and moved the few steps to him before dropping to his knees on the carpet. Chesterton could see the skewer clearly now, red hot, glowing.

It moved out of his line of vision, and Chesterton suddenly realized he was naked except for his boxer shorts and over-the-calf gray socks.

He could no longer see the skewer, but in a searing stab of pain, he could feel it on his chest. He wanted to scream, but the tape covering his mouth made him gag.

THE ROTORTHROB SOUND of the helicopter's blades seemed more pronounced to him now as the Bell Utility Twin moved low over the tree line. Track felt his stomach heave as the helicopter suddenly dipped, skimming the close-cropped grass, settling in beyond Marble Arch in a corner of Hyde Park. Sir Abner Chesterton's apartment was less than four blocks away in Shepherd's Park.

As the forward tip of the runner touched, Track popped open the seat restraint, pushed the cabin door open and ducked as he jumped under the spinning rotors. He glanced back once. Inspector Hall and Tompkins of the Home Office were racing out behind him. Following them came two uniformed officers.

Track could hear Hall shouting to him, "Out of the park and three blocks straight down—should be the far side of the street—but I'll have a car here in under five minutes."

"No time," Track shouted back. He had no gun, his equipment still with his luggage back at Heathrow. He knew that Sir Edward Hall carried one, but couldn't afford to wait.

If Johannes Krieger was with Sir Abner Chesterton, it was for one purpose only—information about the investigation of the theft of the ninety-nine remaining thermonuclear warheads. And after he got the information, or if by some miracle Chesterton was able to hold it back—death!

Track was now out of the park, skidding on his heels. He ran, looking up the street. Out of the corner of his eye, he saw George come up fast beside him. "Just like the Western movies," Track said, panting. "That-a-way!"

A hundred yards, then across the street—that was all the distance that remained. Track recognized the number of the building from Sir Abner's address. His breath came in short gasps as he dodged a truck and reached the middle of the street.

He had to stop for an instant as a van bore down on him. He glanced behind him to see George skirt a classic MG. Hall, Tompkins and the two bobbies were at the curb, coming into the street.

The van passed, and Track brushed a Bentley's rear bumper. He threaded his way between a parked vintage Rover and an Austin Mini, and leaped up the curb.

He half sagged against the frosted-glass doorway of the red brick Victorian apartment house. The door was locked.

"The bell," he heard George pant. "Geez, I smoke too many cigarettes for this stuff."

"We try the bell, Krieger'll know," Track gasped in reply.

There were four bells indicating four apartments, each occupying its own floor. Sir Abner had the top floor, Track remembered.

One of the bobbies was up beside him and Track reached toward the man, grabbing his truncheon. "Gimme that, corporal." Track rammed the club into the glass near the door handle. A jagged hole about the size of a grapefruit appeared. He quickly pushed his arm through, found the inside handle and released the lock.

Withdrawing his hand, he threw his weight against the door, half stumbling inside.

The floors and parts of the walls were composed of tiny segments of sparkling white and deep black tiles in a wainscotting effect.

A massive frosted-glass globe hung from the ceiling and shed a soft glow over the foyer. An elevator encased in ornate brass caging and a winding staircase presented themselves to the left.

Track raced toward the stairs. "This way, hurry," he

shouted, hearing Tompkins barking some sort of order behind him. George and the corporal were nearest to Track as he raced up the staircase three treads at a time.

He reached the first landing, swung around it and continued to climb, his breath short, his shins aching. The elevator would have been too slow, and the noise might have alerted Krieger causing him to kill if he hadn't already.

At the second landing George was outdistancing him. He should, he's twelve years younger, Track told himself.

George was past the landing now running, at such an angle that he appeared to be throwing himself ahead.

Track was taking two steps at a time. His legs aching, his arms pulling him along the handrailing, he reached the landing. The bobby was beside him.

At the top, Track stumbled forward. He saw George already standing beside the door, holding his right shoe, ready to use the heel like a club. Still gasping, Track sagged back against the wall opposite the door and held his hand up to signal two policemen to wait.

Track started for the door, took a long step forward, put his weight on his right foot, and pivoted half right, his left foot snaking up toward the center of the lockplate in a double taekwon-do kick.

As he spun out of the kick, the door burst open and George flew past him.

Track rushed in behind him. A woman, tall and beautiful, held a kitchen skewer. Sir Abner was writhing on the carpet, the scant hair on his chest on fire.

Track felt his jaw set as George dived toward the woman. But the woman, who had to be Johannes Krieger, stepped aside as George hurtled over and landed on Chesterton and smothering the flames on his chest.

Krieger raised his Walther and Track threw himself into a forward roll as the pistol thundered over his head.

As Track came out of the roll at the edge of the coffee table, he saw one of the bobbies go down, and heard a cry of pain.

Track's arm shot up, the edge of his left hand connecting hard against the inside of Krieger's forearm, deflecting the muzzle of the gun. Another shot rang out, and the large rococo mirror above the fireplace exploded into tiny spikes of lethal glass like a fragmentation grenade.

Track's right fist shot forward, the middle knuckles going for the center of the feminine-looking face. The auburn head snapped back, and Track felt a stabbing surge of pain in his groin. He threw himself left as he went down, seeing a second kick miss, its high arc restricted by the tight skirt. Track realized the skirt was all that saved him from having been crippled by the death-merchant's vicious kick.

A pistol coughed from behind him, Sir Edward Hall's Walther PP. Krieger threw himself to the right, and back, and the shot whispered past. Track saw the impact as the chafing dish crashed off the top of the bar behind Krieger. An instant later a sheet of flame rose from behind the bar.

Krieger fired again, and Track heard Sir Edward's voice scream out, "My leg—damn the bloody bastard!"

Two more shots echoed into the room. Bottles behind the bar shattered, and the alcohol fed the flames. Tongues of fire shot up and licked at the ceiling as Track rolled to his right, still doubled up with pain.

He could see George moving, hear him shouting, "You son of a bitch!"

Krieger's gun cracked twice, and George, coming in low, slapped the gunhand out and away from his body.

For an instant it looked absurd as George and Krieger embraced, locked in combat. George's forehead was smeared with blood and sweat.

Track rolled onto his side, his breath finally starting to come back. He looked up as he tried to stand. The ceiling was awash with fire and tiny droplets of flame were showering down onto the carpet.

He could see Hall, himself wounded, struggling with the shot bobby. Now he knew how the vets felt during a fire attack in Nam. Tompkins was getting Sir Abner to his feet, helping him across the burning carpet.

Track stood to his full height. "George!" he shouted.

He started across the room, jumping a burning line of carpet. The sofa was a bed of flames, the far wall by the bar an inferno. George had Krieger against the bar, his right fist hammering into Krieger's body again and again. Suddenly Track realized it was the shoe—George was beating Krieger across the chest and abdomen with the heel of his shoe, using it like a blackjack.

Both men fell, as a chunk of blazing ceiling came down around them.

Track searched frantically through the shimmering wall of flame for his nephew, shouting his name over and over.

And then he saw them. Krieger held a shiny brass fireplace poker aloft in his right hand. As Track watched, helpless to reach George in time, the poker hacked downward. George tried to block it, but the murderous blow screamed down his forearm and glanced off his temple. George fell back, his corded muscles suddenly lifeless and a white pallor spreading over his skin.

Track charged forward, jumping over the flames, feeling the heat as it seared his skin.

Krieger raised the poker again to crash it down on George's head as the senseless man lay in a twisted heap on the rug.

Track's left hand flicked out like the head of a striking rattlesnake, catching the poker in its deathly swing. A sharp stab of pain raced along his arm like an electric current. He twisted his body half-right, his left foot came up and he stabbed a short kick into Krieger's side, doubling Krieger forward. Track was still on the move. He spun more than one-hundred and eighty degrees, away from Krieger and back, the edge of his right hand chopping against Krieger's carotid artery. But the force was insufficient, the reach too great to put the Nazi zealot down.

As Krieger stumbled forward, he lurched toward Track, stabbing the poker at him in a low thrust at death. Track crossed his arms in a classic blocking position and the poker deflected wide of his groin. Track turned away, dragging the poker and Krieger's body with him. His left foot kicked and sank into Krieger's abdomen.

Krieger fell back, releasing the poker. His quick hands shot down to the hem of the skirt, ripping at it, splitting the side seam. A razor-edged stiletto of gleaming steel caught the tint of red and orange from the flames as it flashed into his hand from inside his nylon-stockinged right thigh.

Legs free of the tight skirt, Krieger's right leg kicked out. Track leaped backward out of the way as Krieger wheeled into a second kick, then another and another. Track sidestepped and backstepped until he felt the searing heat of the flames at his back.

Krieger's right foot flashed again, and Track's hand shot out, catching the right ankle. Sidestepping left, Track snapped his right foot twice into Krieger's groin. Track then turned all the way left, twisting the leg, pulling Krieger down.

As Krieger fell past him, Track felt the tingle, then the sharp pain of the stiletto as the blade creased his right bicep.

Krieger was down on the floor, but his left foot kicked up and Track caught the blow full against his abdomen, reeling back with its force.

Krieger was up again and coming, the knife held almost gracefully in his right hand as a fencer would hold a foil. His face was menacing, his lips pulled back into a vicious sneer. There was a flash of movement, and Krieger's body was firing toward him. Track dodged right, feigned a wheeling movement left and hammered his fist into Krieger's stomach.

Krieger reeled back from the force of the blow, then whipped the knife around in a sweeping arc of destruction. Track wheeled 180-degrees right on his left foot, his right kicked against the knife hand, and the stiletto sailed out of Krieger's fist and into the flames.

Track finished the turn and unleashed the heel of his left hand against Krieger's chin. As Krieger spun away from the punch, Track's right fist battered against Krieger's rib cage. The bodice of the black dress was wet and sticky.

Track looked at his knuckles as he snapped back the right, they were red with blood. Krieger's blood.

Krieger stumbled back against a small table, almost losing his balance. His face was contorted with pain and his right arm gripped his left side across his chest. He was like a wounded animal as his eyes darted about the room. He thought only of survival and looked only for escape.

Track reached deep inside himself and summoned up the strength to strike the final blow. And then he heard it, an ominous creaking sound above the roar and hiss of the surrounding conflagration.

He heard Hall's voice yell from beyond the flames, "Track—Dan! The bloody chandelier—the whole ceiling!"

Track looked up. The ceiling was a sea of flames, smoke curled and billowed from it like massive breakers. An enormous crystal chandelier at its center shimmered and listed as it started to rip away from the burning ceiling.

Track looked across the room. Beyond a low wall of flame, George was moving but not getting up, not getting out of the way.

Track ran toward him, his left pantleg on fire.

"George!" he rasped.

In two quick steps he was behind the six-foot-two twenty-five-year-old. With nothing but pure adrenaline pumping through his battered muscles, he picked the big man up and tried to run. The roar of the bonfire around him was pierced only by a sickening tear from above.

"The ceiling. My God, Dan!" screamed Sir Edward Hall from the doorway.

Track stumbled and fell toward the stairs leading down to the entrance hall. Out of the corner of his eye he saw the glittering chandelier. It was falling, as if in slow motion, dragging with it huge pieces of burning ceiling.

On his knees, his nephew cradled in his arms, Track hunched over to shield George's face. Slowly, he edged forward, getting to his feet. Chunks of burning debris crashed around him and sparks smoldered on the fabric of his jacket. The room was dense with thick gray smoke that seared at his lungs. His eyes were stinging, and his face felt as if it was on fire.

Finally, his feet found the stairs leading down and out of the apartment. As he groped his way forward he heard Hall's voice shouting, "Dan! There's a fire ladder by the stairwell!"

He felt arms and hands around him, the burden of George's weight lifted from him.

He fell to his knees, coughing, his eyes streaming, but the smoke less dense. Tompkins and Hall were beside him.

Slowly, Track pushed himself up, coughing, his senses reeling. "Krieger!" He screamed the word back into the apartment, through the roaring wall of flames.

Together, the survivors heard the shattering of glass from inside the apartment, and an instant later a blood-boiling tongue of flame danced and kicked its way through the apartment doorway.

"He must have gone through a window!" said Tompkins.

"Krieger!" Track shouted. "I've got to know where the warheads are!" He made a last desperate attempt to rush the doorway.

Track felt the two Englishmen grab at him and drag him back from the doorway. He strained, staring into the furnace that had once been Sir Abner Chesterton's flat, willing Krieger to stumble through the doorway. Finally, he let himself be taken, dropping forward, supporting himself against the two men.

JOHANNES KRIEGER LOOKED like a bloodied and scorched rag as he hung from the lowest rung of the fire escape at the side of Sir Abner Chesterton's apartment building.

His eyes winced as he tried to fight off the pain.

Two bobbies raced through the alley beneath him, their footsteps echoing crisply in the winter darkness. They didn't look up. He knew some of his ribs were broken. He'd felt that kind of pain before. His hands were cut and swollen from his desperate fight with Track, and his legs were scorched and numb where the fire had fused the nylon stockings onto his skin.

Krieger swung from the fire escape until the two policemen had safely rounded a corner. Then he let go. His knees buckled as he dropped the final twelve feet to the pavement.

He pushed himself up and staggered against the alley wall of the building. He was cold, the back of his dress was ripped half away, the skirt torn up the side seam.

He licked his lips.

Johanna Gruber, his convenient identity as a flight attendant, was dead. He hadn't gotten the information he had come for. Track had fought him to a standoff. The thought crossed his mind that perhaps he had almost made a fatal mistake. He had underestimated Dan Track.

Krieger edged along the wall toward the street.

The sounds coming from the direction of the roadway told him that firemen and policemen were everywhere. Somewhere out there was Dan Track. Waiting for him.

He fell back against the wall, his breathing was heavy and labored, his left side sticky and cold. He could never escape dressed as he was.

Out on the street he saw a single uniformed bobby standing in the glow of the headlights of a police car parked diagonally in the roadway about fifty feet away from the building.

Shielded from view by two large fire trucks that blocked the road at the bottom of the alley, Krieger stumbled toward the unsuspecting officer.

He raised his voice, Johanna Gruber's voice one last time. "Help! Help me, officer. Hurry!" He fell forward and rolled onto his back, waiting.

The young bobby rushed to his side and bent over him. As he raised his whistle to signal for aid, Krieger's left hand snapped up, his open palm ramming against the base of the bobby's nose. He saw shock register in the young man's eyes and felt the ethmoid bone splinter beneath his blow.

The policeman died instantly, his brain punctured.

Krieger was on his feet, dragging the young officer into the shadows like a lion with a fresh kill.

He whipped Johanna Gruber's wig from his head and stripped away the remains of her clothes. Within a minute he was ready to face the world again, a member of the London constabulary.

He allowed a smile to cross his lips, despite the pain in his side.

TRACK SAT ON THE CURB across the street from the burning apartment building and watched his nephew.

George had been lucky. He was going to need some proper care, but he was going to be all right. Track had already outlived his sister; he had no intention of outliving her only son.

A bobby ran up to Sir Edward Hall. Hall was on an ambulance gurney, his leg bandaged, but still in command. "Sir," the man reported, "the building is evacuated. Everyone is accounted for except that Krieger chap the American gentleman mentioned."

"He's alive, officer. Don't worry about Krieger," Track rasped. He wanted a Cuesta-Rey Six T, but didn't think his lungs would take the smoke.

Sir Edward turned to look at Track. "You mentioned something back there about warheads. Stolen warheads?"

Track shrugged his shoulders. "All that smoke was getting to me," he replied.

"Why are you after Krieger?" Hall was sitting up, his face registering pain.

Track started to speak, but Sir Abner Chesterton's voice cut him off. Track looked up. Chesterton, wrapped in a blanket, looked as though he was shivering. His voice low, he said, "I'd intended to give you at least a partial briefing. Apparently it'll have to be now."

"Briefing?" Hall looked up at Chesterton.

Track watched Chesterton's eyes. "Yes," he said, "but before that, you must contact MI6 to see if the Americans have tipped anything to the secret service."

"Secret Intelligence Service?" quizzed Hall. "What the devil would SIS have to do with all this?" He waved his arm toward the still-burning apartment house.

Track crouched down beside Hall's gurney. "Sir Edward," he whispered. "A few months ago there were one hundred thermonuclear warheads—each 500-kilotons—being taken to a central servicing area in New Mexico to have defective detonators replaced. Each one had the explosive force of five-hundred-thousand tons of TNT all going off at once in an area not much bigger than a large suitcase. Krieger and his gang of neo-Nazi terrorists intercepted the shipment and stole them all. Sir Abner, George here—" he gestured toward his nephew, now standing behind him "—and I got one back in Chicago. Ninety-nine are left."

"Good·God, man," said an incredulous Hall.

Track grinned. "But don't tell anybody until you get clearance," he cautioned.

Track looked up at Sir Abner, who was standing beside him. He wondered how the dignified older man must feel after having been taken in so completely by Krieger.

Track started to say something, when he heard the shrillness of police whistles coming from down the street to his right, near the alley that ran alongside the burning apartment building.

Suddenly he was up, and started to run. Chesterton was beside him.

Ahead, he could see Tompkins, and around him a knot of uniformed officers. Track broke through and stood beside Tompkins.

Lying in the alley, a fire-department paramedic beside him, was a young man. That he was dead was obvious. The body, oddly pink against the blackness of the alley, was stripped naked. Not far away, hanging from a trash can, was a bloodstained woman's slip, a torn dress and an auburn wig.

Track felt motion beside him and turned. It was Hall, two bobbies supporting him on his injured leg.

Hall whispered, "My God. Krieger has escaped—as one of us."

Tompkins spoke. "I've ordered the entire area sealed off."

Track turned a grim smile on the counterterrorist specialist of the Home Office. "What the hell good does that do?" he demanded as anger swelled up inside him. "If you've got cops cordoning off the area, it's better than even money Krieger is one of them. He's probably killed someone else by now and taken a fresh set of clothes. He could be anybody. He's so good he could be one of us," he cried.

Track wanted to strike out at somebody. Hard.

**3**

The Zurich airport was crowded, but Track, as he moved away from customs with his stuff sack over his shoulder and his flight bag and attaché case in his hands, wasn't worried that he'd miss his driver. A moment later he saw him, hulking above the menagerie of tourists and business travelers, a head above the tallest person Track could see. He had apparently taken to shaving his head. Either that or he had suffered some dramatic hair loss.

Track knew that Zulu saw him. But Zulu remained motionless, like a misplaced colossus. His skin was the color of expensive dark Swiss chocolate.

Track threaded his way through the crowd and stopped three feet in front of Zulu. Track was at least ten inches shorter. "I'd say it's good to see you again," he said, "but why base a relationship on lies?"

"I might well say the same, Major Track," replied Zulu. "Miss Desiree has sent me to collect you."

The voice was a deep rumble, sounding as if it came up from the depths of the earth.

Track tensed as Zulu suddenly reached out with his left hand. But it was to take the flight bag rather than take life, and Track released it to him.

"I have a car waiting for us. I suggest we get on." Zulu turned and started through the crowd, as if oblivious to it, cutting a wedge through the traffic. Track followed closely in the monstrous man's wake.

"Will it bother you if I smoke a cigar?" Track asked once they got into the maroon Mercedes.

Zulu didn't answer as he pressed the power-window button and Track's front-seat window on the passenger-side went down three inches.

"If you would be more comfortable, I can pull off to the side for a moment and help you transfer to the rear seat," Zulu's stentorian voice boomed.

"No," demured Track, "it's more friendly riding up here with you. Anyway, I've seen too many spy movies where the glass partition comes up between the front and rear seats and the hermetically sealed rear compartment fills with cyanide gas or something."

Zulu raised an eyebrow as he turned a reproving glance on Track. But he said nothing and looked away.

Track studied his actions for a moment as he guillotined the end from a thin, dark Cuesta Rey Six-T before lighting it with his Zippo.

"How is she?" Track asked after a while.

There was no need to say her name. Both men knew who they were talking about. Desiree Goth, a slinky, sexy arms dealer had smuggled her way into Track's life almost four years ago. He had been Major Track then, with the Army's Criminal Investigation Division. He was on the verge of arresting her for arms smuggling when she unexpectedly ambushed his heart. Since then, they had been apart more often than they were together. But when they were together, they were never very far apart.

It was a long moment before Zulu spoke. "Miss Desiree is well, major," he finally said. "If anything, her beauty has increased since you last saw her. And you, major, I noticed an article of your apparel. The Null belt buckle. Is your employer once again the United States government?"

Track looked down at the rectangular bronze buckle at his midsection. Ken Null's buckles had become almost an unofficial badge of the Company and other clandestine U.S. governmental agencies.

Track looked back at Zulu. "Null made me a holster, shoulder rig," he said. "I saw the buckle and I liked it, so I wear it. And I don't work for the government. But that's it, isn't it?" Track smiled, inhaling on the cigar, watching as Zulu threaded the Mercedes through a knot of traffic and into the clear again. "You think I'm here to arrest Desiree, right? But I'm not."

"You cannot arrest her in Switzerland," replied Zulu calmly. "And you came through customs too quickly to be legally armed. Yet I know there are ways to evade metal detectors. Perhaps you have come to play a more dangerous game."

"Kill Desiree?" There were no flies on Track as he watched the big black man's face set hard. "Why would I do that?"

Zulu exhaled long and hard. "There have been two attempts on her life recently," he said. "The first was merely a hazard of the trade. A disgruntled low bidder sent a talentless assassin to compensate Miss Desiree for not selling him the arms he required. The second, however, was the official emissary of a European nation. The first man I killed with my shotgun. The second man Miss Desiree forbade me to kill. We sent him back to his embassy with his broken legs properly splinted. Since then I have had reason to suspect that others might come, others with official sanction."

Track stared out the window and listened to the slipstream whistle behind them.

Finally he asked, "Then why doesn't she get out of the international arms trade? She's made enough money to live like a princess for the rest of her life."

"Miss Desiree," Zulu began as Track turned to look at him, "has not confided this reason to me, and it is, of course, not my position to inquire of her."

It was the end of the conversation, like a bell dinging, Track thought. His mind drifted back to the events in

London a week ago. George had mended well, but the doctors had warned him to take it easy for a while. Sir Edward Hall was on crutches, but he too would recover. Sir Abner Chesterton's pride hurt more than any of his wounds, and he went around blaming himself for the whole debacle.

Then he thought of Johannes Krieger and his lips tightened. Krieger was a scum, a megalomaniac bent on one course. He would either crush the innocent people of the world under his jackbooted heel, or he would tear them apart in the process. But not if Dan Track had anything to say about it.

DESIREE GOTH STOOD MOTIONLESS in front of her dressing-room mirror. Her rich black hair tumbled down to her bare shoulders. She admired her body. She was proud of it, proud of the things it could do.

She picked up a pair of gray linen slacks from the chair beside the mirror and began to slip them on. Her legs were long and well-shaped, the thighs firm and the skin taut over her sinewy muscles. Her calves tapered down to slim ankles.

She pulled the waistband over her narrow hips, the pants hugging her behind and snuggling into her crotch. Her stomach was smooth and firm beneath her hands as she buttoned the pants. She worked hard at staying in peak condition.

Next came a pink zephyr's-wool sweater with a V-neck and dolman sleeves. For some reason, she always felt freer and easier in its bulky, loose-fitting form. As she raised her arms to pull it on, she caught the profile of her breasts in the mirror. They were full and firm, the pure white skin extending to large pink nipples.

She slipped the sweater over her head and felt the fine wool brush tantalizingly against her skin. She tossed her head and shook her shiny hair free of the neckline.

Around her long slender neck she wore a finely sculpted platinum necklace. Just a hint of makeup highlighted her aristocratic features. Her high cheekbones, the ones that could have made her a million-dollar-a-year fashion model, showed just a slight blush of pink. Her lips were full and red and inviting. Her light-blue eyes were bright but distant, as if she were suddenly focusing on the next few hours.

Her tongue played on her lips.

"Dan," she whispered to her own reflection. A sparkle flashed in her eyes when she said his name.

THEY HAD DRIVEN ALONG the finger of the Lake of Zurich on a road that extended toward Liechtenstein, near the Austrian border. Once out of heavier traffic, Zulu had maintained the Mercedes at just below seventy miles per hour. The Rolex Sea Dweller on Track's left wrist indicated that nearly an hour had elapsed.

The road had taken them up into the mountains, where it presented startling vistas. Classic picture-book wooden chalets with carved ornate fronts clung to the mountainsides around them like the spots of a connect-the-dot drawing he had worked as a kid.

He didn't look at Zulu as he asked him, "How much longer, do you suppose?"

"Another five minutes, major," replied Zulu. Track could detect the emphasis on the final word.

"It's mister, you know," shot back Track. "I haven't been a major for a while."

"Yes, but we colonial blacks cling to such titles of authority and prestige in dealing with whites, like a touchstone amid the insecurity of twentieth-century life." Zulu's Oxford-educated accent was a bit stronger now.

Track looked at Desiree's bodyguard, confidant and business manager. "No shit, huh? Well, then you have a special dispensation. Go ahead and call me major. I wouldn't want to cause you any mental anguish or anything like that," Track allowed.

"It is not my position, of course, but as regards Miss Desiree...." Zulu shifted his gaze from the road to Track as he spoke, Track watching him.

"Are my intentions honorable toward her?" Track's voice inflected with the words, he was amused and mildly shocked.

"Perhaps not in those exact words, but the spirit is there, yes," Zulu said.

"It depends on what one considers honorable, doesn't it?" Track knew it was a little silly, but he didn't want to give Zulu the satisfaction of a straight answer.

Track flicked his cigar out the window.

A cuckoo clock turned dollhouse, but raised to adult scale, came immediately into view. The last time he had seen Desiree Goth she had not owned this house.

He stepped out of the Mercedes onto the white-graveled driveway and took it all in, the security fences, the discreet guardhouses, the landscaping designed for privacy. He had just turned his attention to the front of the house itself when one of a pair of dark double doors swung open. A figure stood in the doorway, stealing the brilliance away from the setting sun.

Desiree Goth.

Track started to walk toward her. She stood just inside the doorway for an instant longer, then started through, across the shallow granite of the wide top step.

He stopped, still several yards from the steps, staring at this fascinatingly beautiful creature who stood at the base of the steps, her hands hugging her shoulders with her arms crossed over her chest.

Track realized he had been holding his breath. As he exhaled, he saw steam rise from his lips.

"Desiree," he called out.

"Dan," she responded, "come put your arms around me before I take a chill. Please."

Track walked up to her.

Her hair shone, rich, dark and full. Her eyes, as blue as the winter sky, held him like a vise.

He drew her close to him. She was doing it, what she always could do.

Track kissed her hard, tasting her mouth, wanting to devour her.

Desiree responded.

## 4

The younger of the two Americans, the one called George Beegh, had a concussion and had been in hospital for observation, Krieger had learned through his sources in London's right-wing terrorist underground. Krieger wished he had killed him. The other one, the ex-Army CID major, Dan Track, had flown to Zurich, Switzerland, to confer with someone unknown. Krieger supposed it would be Desiree Goth, the arms broker. His dossier on Track revealed that some years back Track and Desiree Goth had had an affair and that they were still close. Krieger smiled. For an instant he envied Track. Krieger had seen Desiree Goth once—she was exquisite. But Krieger doubted whether the rather mercenary Mademoiselle Goth would risk alienating trusted contacts in the underground movements throughout Europe by attempting to aid Track in obtaining information.

Sir Abner Chesterton, the Englishman who represented the Consortium, the largest of the multinational insurance underwriters, and employed Track and George Beegh, was alive and well and would likely be leaving England soon. The old fool.

His back turned against a seventeenth-century fresco of the Virgin and John beneath the cross, Krieger rested his bearded chin in his left hand as he "meditated" in the small chamber at the side of the Greek Orthodox church's elaborate narthex.

He studied the wristwatch he had pinned under the flowing black cossack he wore. It was time to go.

He stood slowly, as befit his years, adjusting the set of his flat-crowned miter.

He hunched forward slightly as he walked with the support of a walking stick. He nodded and raised his right hand in blessing as he passed out of the narthex amid a throng of women. They were professional mourners. One day he would provide the stupid women with something they could really mourn over.

Krieger moved ahead into the narrow cobbled street, turned to his right and walked down the slight hill.

He thread his way along the maze of noisy streets for ten minutes, and soon he could see the night blackness of the Sea of Crete stretched out below him like a sinister abyss. The sleazy quay-side cafés acted as a buffer between the blackness of the water and the dingy grayness of the nighttime Rethimnone itself.

Krieger skirted the open front of the nearest of the cafés, returning the smiles and good wishes of the revelers as they noticed him, the old priest. The clinking of glasses and the high-pitched, forced laughter of young girls who sat with dark-faced, mustachioed young men fought for precedence over the blaring Western rock music.

There were several boats on the small harbor, but one in particular caught his eye. On it stood a woman.

The blond-haired, deeply tanned beauty was clothed in a faded red top, which covered her little more than a bra would, and a skirt that looked to be nothing more than a piece of brightly printed material wrapped around her waist and trailing unevenly to midcalf. She ran her hands through her hair as he walked past the deck on which she stood, looking down on him.

She reached down suddenly, the red scarf in her left hand matching the red of the top that held her breasts. In an instant, the scarf covered her hair and she was moving away from him, toward the stern of the ship with its single main mast. The ship was a brilliant white, and looked freshly painted.

Krieger kept walking, past more of the seemingly endless cafés to his right, and fishing boats to his left. The Sea of Crete stretched beyond in the darkness.

He could feel someone behind him as he turned into the streets again, and he stopped in the first doorway sufficiently dark to offer good cover. He hitched up the hem of his cassock and reached up beneath his pantleg. A black-handled, black-bladed Gerber Mark 1 fighting knife, its cat's-paw handle tightly curled in his fingers, slid into view.

She called herself Marlena Fields these days, but when he had first known her in Germany it had been Marlene Wellman. Like himself, she was a Nazi. But he trusted no one; it was implicit in his every thought. And so he waited in the sticky, hot darkness, holding his breath as she walked past.

"Marlena," he whispered hoarsely.

She turned abruptly on her right heel. She wore red sandals that were laced around her calves with red leather thongs.

"It is you!" she exclaimed toward the darkness.

"Come here," he called.

She stepped into the doorway. He smelled her perfume.

"Johannes...all of this," and she gestured to his outfit. "I had feared that you...."

It was worth the risk. He drew her toward him, still holding the knife, his mouth crushing down against hers. He felt the moisture of her lips, smelled her breath. She tasted of the kind of ouzo that became addictive. Her body pushed against him. He could feel the firmness of her breasts through her thin top and the heat of her loins as her body molded to his.

"Johannes," she sighed.

"Is it the boat that we take?" he asked after a moment.

"Too slow, I think. My car is nearby," she replied.

"Tell me where and I will follow after you at a distance," Krieger instructed her.

"The third intersection up the hill, then walk to your right, Joannes," she said. "The car is an old green Fiat with a taillight missing—the left or the right one, I don't really remember."

"If there is anyone around, I will walk along the street and you can intercept me when it is safe. Now, quickly, go ahead," he urged her.

Her green eyes stared up into his, and he bent over her and kissed her hard, kissed her fast.

She whispered, "I'll be glad when you take off your disguise. The beard." She laughed. "It tickles me, you know?"

She walked away, and Johannes Krieger watched as she navigated the cobbled street in her ridiculous sandals with their spike-thin high heels.

He palmed the knife up his sleeve rather than sheath it on his leg under the cassock.

He waited for several minutes, until she was well ahead of him. Then he stepped out of the doorway. A young woman was staring at him. His Greek excellent, his accent perfect, he began, "Are you alone?"

"Yes," she answered, nodding.

He looked up and down the street. She was indeed alone.

"Come here," he said with a smile, gesturing toward the doorway.

She looked at him, her eyes wide in the moonlight. She nodded as she stepped past him. Looking puzzled, she asked, "Are you all right?" He nodded.

"Everything is okay?" she insisted.

"Yes, everything is all right," he said and rammed the spear-pointed blade of his knife into her throat, ripping down to sever the carotid artery.

He let the body slump away from him against the doorway wall, as her heart still pumped and the wounds sprayed blood.

Krieger turned out of the doorway, the knife blade wiped clean across the front of the dead woman's white blouse. He walked up the hill, following Marlena Fields.

THERE HAD BEEN A DRIVE of more than an hour along a barren and winding road paralleling the coastline, and the descent to the water itself had been perilous in darkness. Marlena had removed her sandals and gone barefoot.

He hitched up the hem of the cassock as he waded, barefoot too and his pantslegs rolled up, into the surf toward a darkly colored two-seater rowboat. The black-haired man who sat in the rear by the oarlocks fought the waves. Krieger assumed he was the pilot of the plane that waited a hundred yards beyond the surf.

Krieger looked at the frail craft. "This will carry us?" he asked Marlena.

"Yes, Johannes," came her reply.

He settled into the front seat, facing Marlena and the man he presumed to be the pilot.

"Herr Krieger." The man nodded as he extended his right hand. Krieger took it briefly. "I am honored, sir, just to meet you," continued the man. "I am Yannis Lemoronos, and I am at your service, sir."

"What kind of boat is this?" demanded Krieger.

"The Americans make it," Lemoronos reported. "They call it a Porta-Bote. When we reach the seaplane I will unlock the oars, remove the seats and the boat folds to the size of a large surfboard. There is provision to secure it beneath the fuselage of my aircraft, Herr

Krieger. It is a very useful boat for a pilot like me.'' He smiled.

Krieger clamped his hands to the gunwales. He hated boats of any kind, and one that folded made him all the more nervous.

The flight took less than a half hour, the time to fold out the Porta-Bote and refit the seats less than two minutes, Marlena helping Yannis. Krieger was again at the prow as the boat was rowed to the shore of an island, small enough to be rarely visited, rarely noticed on maps of the fringe area of the Cyclades.

He stepped firmly from the rowboat and into the surf, and from the black rocks beyond the narrow white beach, men appeared.

Krieger walked toward them, noting their weapons—Uzi submachine guns, AR-18 automatic rifles.

He stopped, just beyond the furtherest lapping of the surf, feeling Marlena beside him.

He addressed the men who stood staring at him, their weapons held diagonally across their chests. ''I am Johannes Krieger. Soon, I will be in the halls of power, and only I shall wield the power. The mighty ones of all nations will yield to me because of this. And I shall lead the world into a new era of glory, the glory that was robbed from our world during the atrocity of 1944.

''But I shall counter atrocity with atrocity. Of the ninety-nine remaining 500-kiloton warheads, seventy-four are still within the continental United States and under the direction of Klaus Gurnheim, a master explosives expert. Some of these will be transported to strategic locations in Mexico and Canada, as well.

''Of the twenty-five in Europe, twenty-four will be planted throughout the NATO and Warsaw Pact nations. The twenty-fifth I myself shall see to. It will be an object lesson that the world shall never forget. The same effect I had originally planned for the American city of

Chicago, but this time even more glorious, more spectacular. And I shall see to it personally.

"Marlena will guide you in your individual and collective tasks. Under my direction, individual task outlines will soon be prepared. These you will memorize and then destroy in my presence."

He reached out, holding Marlena's right hand in his left, then raised their hands high.

Johannes Krieger watched as the men of the night bowed their heads. He could hear nothing but the lapping of the surf at his feet.

5

It was cold enough that the children could skate again, and Sergei Baslovitch stared at them through his frosted window. He smudged at the frost on one of the panes of glass with the heel of his right fist. Now he could see more clearly, but the view was still distorted.

He turned away and walked the few paces to his desk. He sat down and looked at the sheafs of reports, picked up one, then threw it down. He stood again and lighted a long filtered Stolichyne, inhaling the strong tobacco smoke. He preferred American cigarettes or British-made Players, over the strong, dry Russian tobacco.

Sergei Baslovitch walked back to the window, pocketing the old Ronson lighter as he went. He looked out across Dzerzhinsky Square far to his left, to Children's World. He thought of his own childhood on a dingy street near the ribbon of the Yauza River as it threaded between the outskirts of Moscow and the Moscow River itself. "A long way to here," he said in English. At the Chicago School run by the KGB, he had distinguished himself in his study of languages, but he had always been terrible at learning how to blow things up.

Sergei Baslovitch stared back at his desk, taking a long drag on the cigarette. *"Merde,"* he whispered. French had been a good language for him as well.

He walked back across his small office and sat down.

Reports. He much preferred reading technical data in German, it was more precise. These were in Russian, from agents operating inside the United States and

England. They told him there was some connection between the Consortium, the cartel of international insurance underwriters, and the wreck of a subway train in Chicago. Terrorists, Baslovitch wondered. None that he knew. The thought amused him. With the concerted efforts of the KGB to bankroll and hence control international terrorism, it was almost refreshing to encounter a group that was still somewhat of an enigma.

His telephone buzzed and he picked it up. "Baslovitch," he said.

The caller was his immediate superior, Colonel Yehrevhenskiy. "Yes, comrade," Baslovitch answered. He hung up the phone.

He stood up, stubbing out his cigarette beside the dozen or so others.

He stepped to the small picture-framed mirror. He needed a shave, his five-o'clock shadow was at its worst for him. He smoothed back his sandy-brown hair, then straightened the brown woolen tie he had bought in London. He found his Harris Tweed sportscoat and shrugged into it as he started from the office.

Colonel Yehrevhenskiy ushered him through the door and closed it without himself entering.

Baslovitch inhaled, then exhaled hard. He could smell vodka and cigarettes, and it was evident as he walked toward the conference table that moments earlier others had been in the room besides the waiting Ghermahnyevitch, head of the covert-operations section. Ghermahnyevitch meant "son of Germany." It was a stupid-sounding name and obviously a manufactured one.

Baslovitch approached the near end of the conference table, farthest from Ghermahnyevitch.

He said nothing but *"zdras tivooytye,"* standing erect but not at attention. He was not in uniform and Ghermahnyevitch had no military rank.

Finally, the thin-faced, dark-eyed man sitting at the far

end of the table looked up, the dome of skin that crowned his head a waxy color in the poor overhead yellow light.

"You can practice your English with me, Baslovitch. And is it a good evening?"

"Yes, comrade," responded Sergei, "a good evening it looks to be."

"You have been studying this affair with the derailment of the train in Chicago in the United States," Ghermahnyevitch continued.

"Yes, comrade," Baslovitch said automatically.

"You explained to Colonel Yehrevhenskiy that you thought it was part of some terrorist conspiracy, and that there is some link with Sir Abner Chesterton and the Consortium, did you not?" stated the Covert Operations officer.

"Yes, comrade," agreed Baslovitch.

"We have reports, which you have not the clearance to see on a routine basis," Ghermahnyevitch informed him. He looked down for a moment, then looked up, his eyes piercing. "These reports indicate that perhaps there has been a rather interesting turn of events for our American friends. The theft of one hundred 500-kiloton nuclear warheads. We wish to know if this is true. Perhaps it is merely a clever ploy to supply us with misleading information while the Americans transfer one hundred warheads to some new strategic site for retargeting. It cannot be said.

"Since you have expressed such interest, and since you are so gifted with languages as to travel anywhere and make yourself seem a native, this job is yours."

Sergei Baslovitch didn't recall expressing any such interest. He had merely been following Yehrevhenskiy's orders. But he said nothing. "If the warheads have been stolen," continued Ghermahnyevitch, "you must obtain at least one for our scientists to study. I believe you have contacts in the right-wing terrorist movement."

"It was Captain Vilnyeva who had these contacts," corrected Baslovitch, "in Italy. But I was introduced to only one such contact. Vilnyeva's operation was something of which I was never informed, comrade."

Baslovitch realized his palms were sweating. He knew the operation, though he had never suspected it at the time. Its intent disgusted him and he was inwardly pleased that it had failed. There were some things, he privately believed, that should not be done.

"Yes," countered Ghermahnyevitch, "but you will leave for Cortina d'Ampezzo immediately, to reestablish this line of contact."

"Perhaps I could consult with Vilnyeva," Baslovitch suggested.

"Vilnyeva is no longer in the hospital," Ghermahnyevitch said firmly. "He is dead. You had not been informed?"

"No, comrade," said Baslovitch. Somehow he was not surprised.

"You are now informed. The hopes of the Russian people go with you." Ghermahnyevitch averted his eyes, turning to the papers littering his end of the long conference table.

The smell of vodka and the heat in the room was stifling.

Baslovitch murmured, "Yes, comrade," and turned and walked away. Colonel Yehrevhenskiy's secretary would have the paperwork, the tickets, the name of the contact who would supply him with the weapons that would be dispatched through the diplomatic pouch for his use.

He knew the drill very well. He listened to his heels click on the hard floor as he walked out of the conference room.

## 6

A Japanese screen made of eight yellowed segments covered the center section of the far wall at the head of the circular staircase that led to the black-and-white checkerboard tile of the hall below. Dan Track tugged at the vest of his new blue suit and started down the stairs.

He'd had a chance to freshen up and he was looking forward to the rest of the night with anticipation. He felt good in the trim cut of the British-made suit. His other one had been destroyed during the deadly combat at Sir Abner Chesterton's flat. But tonight he would try not to think of Krieger.

Desiree waited for him in the library. She stood beside a small mahogany bar at the end of the green-carpeted room. It was more a man's room than a woman's, rich in leather and heavy carvings in the ornate woodwork. She would have bought the walls and moved them here, he realized. No one made rooms like this anymore, regardless of the price offered.

She turned to face him, and it was calculated, he knew, to give him the full impact. She began to walk toward him.

She was wearing a white linen dress that seemed to defy gravity, barely touching her shoulders. A high waist was gathered in the front beneath and between her breasts, and the dress seemed to move like a wave as she walked, encompassing her down to the barely visible toes of her white shoes.

A diamond bracelet glittered at her wrist instead of her Rolex. Small diamond earrings pierced her ears, and a thin necklace of diamonds guarded her throat.

Her glossy hair was swept up at the nape, and as she turned her head slightly to her right he thought he caught the fire of diamonds binding up the rich blackness of her hair.

"What can I say?" He felt himself smile.

"That I'm beautiful?" she teased.

"But you already know that," he said.

"Exquisite, then. You've called me that before," she cooed. "It's rather like being a jewel, isn't it?"

"You should know, kid," Track shot back.

"Why do you call me that?" she asked, as she moved beside him and kissed him lightly on the cheek. She took his left arm, hooking both her hands in the bend of his elbow and walked him toward the small bar. "Why do you call me that—kid?" she repeated.

"I don't know," said Track. "After all, you're not that much younger than I am."

He looked at her and laughed as she feigned a pout. "Well, I feel young, anyway," she smiled. She led him to a leather-covered barstool, and he sat down. Desiree walked behind the bar.

"What would you like, Dan?" she asked coyly.

"To drink?" he asked in return.

"Yes. For now, at least, what would you like to drink?"

"How about soy sauce with a twist and hold the mayo?" he joked.

"I'm serious," she said with a laugh. It was a nice laugh, and Track remembered the few occasions when he'd heard it.

"All right, do you have something as pedestrian as Seagrams Seven?" he asked her.

"I have Canadian Club," she offered.

"Fine," said Track. "I'll have a double shot over ice with a splash—and you can still hold the mayo."

She smiled at him and turned away to a large mahogany and silver tantalus that stood on the ledge behind her. When she turned back she held a decanter in each hand. They looked like the Waterford crystal Track had seen in a magazine once, and around the neck of each decanter was a little sterling silver plaque on a sterling silver chain identifying the contents.

"What happens if the little necklaces get mixed up?" he asked her. "On the bottles, I mean?"

"Then I have to taste everything to tell what it is," she quickly responded.

"Next time it happens, gimme a ring and I'll be on the next plane over," he said with a smile.

"Here." She added the splash to his drink, then handed it across the bar to him.

She poured from the second decanter.

"What are you drinking?" Track inquired.

She set down the decanter and answered. "What else," she said, "but Napoleon Brandy?"

Track leaned forward, taking her right hand in his, touching his lips to her fingertips. "Sometimes you're hard to take," he laughed. But there were other times, he knew...

"I THOUGHT the family dining room would be more intimate," she said to Track. A butler pushed in her chair, and then began to pour wine.

Track looked above the table to a chandelier, small but impressively obvious as crystal. He thought he'd seen enough chandeliers lately to last him a lifetime.

"What do you call this kind of table?" he asked her.

"A Regency table, that's all," she replied.

"I know it's terribly rude," he began, catching a

glimpse of the Beaujolais label on the wine bottle, "but isn't all this, well. . . ."

"Expensive?" she said for him.

"Yeah," said Track.

"Yes, it is," said Desiree, holding her chin high. "But I enjoy it."

"Is that why you stay in the business," Track wanted to know, "to support your tastes?"

"Not really," Desiree conceded. "I could live like this for five lifetimes if I were to quit today. But now that we seem to be talking business, how is it that you think I possibly could help with these allegedly missing missiles?"

"Warheads," Track corrected.

"Yes, warheads. One hundred of them, I believe? Let's see now, at 500-kilotons each, that's roughly a two-and-one-half-mile-diameter fireball, the fireball moving with a high-pressure shock wave, the air catching fire, then heat and infrared light waves. And within about a mile or so of the burst, heat in excess of a thousand calories per centimeter of area. Thirty miles away the heat would flash upward of three-hundred calories for a short duration. At ground zero, millions of degrees Fahrenheit. Does that encompass the spirit of the thing, Dan?" she said. She wasn't showing off. She was deadly serious.

Track sipped at his wine. "Yes," he answered solemnly, "yes, it does."

After a pause, Desiree said, "Are you really very hungry? I'm sure the staff would enjoy the dinner instead, and later I could make us sandwiches."

There was a welcoming softness in her voice. Earlier, Track had told her what had happened in London. She understood how it affected him. She wanted to help him, be there for him.

HER HANDS HAD ALREADY OPENED his vest and his shirt beneath it. Her fingers played on his chest as they stood together in the center of her bedroom.

Yellow light diffused through the shades of the bed-side lamps, giving an incandescent glow to the pink and beige chevroned wallpaper behind her bed. The bed itself was perfectly feminine, from the lace-trimmed dust ruffle and pillowcases to the lace coverlet spread over the shimmering satin of the gold colored goose-down quilt. A floral-patterned bedspread covered the foot of the bed, the flowers nearly the color of her eyes.

She kissed his chest. "You've gotten more gray hairs on your chest since the last time, Dan," she whispered.

"From constantly thinking about you, that's what does it," he said.

He felt her hands at his belt. "Are you in the CIA these days or just pretending—the Null belt buckle, I mean," she inquired.

"What, you and Zulu have the same writer or something?" Track laughed.

She laughed, too. "Maybe, but I've seen the buckle before."

He let her undo it. His own hands searched for the zipper at the back of her dress and found it. He drew her close to him as he ran the zipper down its full length. Under his hands she felt naked even with her cool silk underwear.

She stepped back from him, shrugged her shoulders and moved her hips very slightly. The dress fell to the floor, exposing her high heeled, silk-stockinged legs.

The stockings stayed up, somehow defying gravity like the dress had. But they too were doomed to fall, he realized, just like the dress. He drew her close again, feeling her hands exploring his crotch. . . .

She was straddling him, moving as her hands pressed

against his chest. His palms massaged the nipples of her breasts, feeling them erect against his skin. She tensed against him, and he felt as if he would break, rolling over with her, almost falling together off the bed. Desiree's head was thrown back, her eyes half closed and her lips upturned in a smile warmer than he'd ever seen. Her hair flowed over the side of the bed.

Her legs folded around his hips, and Track thrust his body against hers, feeling the pressure of her legs as they tightened around him. Her hands were moving now, clutching his buttocks, and he could feel her long nails as they stabbed into his flesh.

Together, their bodies shuddered and then relaxed. After a time of lying quietly in each other's arms, they started over again.

DESIREE SAT AT the wooden vanity.

"I like to sit here and brush my hair," she said to him without turning. The makeup mirror in the bathroom is better, but somehow I like this."

Track watched her from the bed. Pale sunlight filtered through the French doors at the far side of the room, and he was reminded of their first night and morning together. Another house, another time.

She wore a plain white satin robe. Its whiteness made the rich blackness of her hair all the more striking as he watched her brush it.

She turned to him and spoke again. "I'll help you find these warheads. Truce until then. Truce off after we find them."

"I've got to get them and return them to the United States government," Track intoned.

"I know that, but I could make an incredible fortune if I stole them from you and sold them to Third World nations," she said with a sly grin.

"Then where will you build your next house—I mean after the world is blown up?" Track asked.

"I don't know," she said as she swiveled on the dainty chair beside the vanity. He could see her face in the mirror. "But I'll always give you my address. And my bed will always be your bed."

Dan Track didn't know what to say.

## 7

"That is St. Anton's principal claim to fame, Mein Herr," the driver said in broken but understandable English.

Miles Jefferson answered, "That's very nice," and followed the driver's pointing arm to a steep, snow-covered mountain.

The Audi kept moving along the plowed road, heavy snow piled in steep banks on either side of the route from Innsbruck. "Yeah," said the driver with evident pride, as if he himself had built the mountain, "that is the Kandahar. Some say it is the greatest of the downhill runs because it has everything."

"That a fact?" Miles Jefferson said, not interested in mountains. "How far is St. Anton, then?"

"Only a few more minutes, Mein Herr."

"Thanks," Jefferson grunted, and looked at his two companions. Special Agent David Palms sat next to him. Special Agent Ed Bartolinski sat in the front seat beside the driver. Jefferson looked out the window, seeing the snow but not seeing it. Jefferson had been given a special presidential directive to leave the United States to pursue a man who lived outside St. Anton. Ultimately, Jefferson was after Johannes Krieger, a fiendish master terrorist. Recently he had learned through contacts in the NSA that to find Krieger he needed to contact the man who was the living connection of all terrorist lines in the right wing, one Abdul al-Kafir.

"What is it that you gentlemen do?" the driver asked.

"Security planning," Miles Jefferson answered. He couldn't very well say he was in the FBI, that he had been given carte blanche as to conduct, and that in the bottom of his suitcase were concealed weapons. And it wasn't really his suitcase at all, it had been left in an airport locker for him with some other items.

This cloak-and-dagger undercover stuff was just the sort of thing that could ruin his political potential and that upset him. "Shit," he murmured.

"What'd you say, Miles," Palms asked absently.

"I was just considering my future," muttered Miles. He smiled at his colleague, but he wasn't smiling inside. The congressional seat he'd been asked to run for was looking less and less of a reality for him with each passing mile.

After all, he thought, if he had wanted to chase around Europe after terrorists he could have joined the CIA or one of the government's more secret clandestine operations. And a black FBI agent in the Austrian Alps wasn't exactly inconspicuous.

"Shit," he muttered again.

Miles Jefferson hated snow.

TRACK SAT ON THE EDGE of the hotel room's double bed, Desiree Goth beside him. Off to one side, George straddled a ladder-back chair. Zulu had brought him to Desiree's home from Zurich, and they had all driven into Austria together. All three were watching Zulu as he set down his gin and tonic and turned to the suitcase beside him on a small table. From his trouser pocket he took out something the size of a handcuff key on a ring and inserted it into the base of an upended pigskin bag. He began to unscrew the brass glides.

Track sipped at his own drink. This time it was really Seagrams Seven. But George had been disappointed. In all of St. Anton, Austria, there was not a single bottle of Jack Daniels Black Label to be had.

Zulu had the bottom of the suitcase open, the base slid aside. From the inside he produced four pistols, one after the other, all identical. Track recognized the handguns as Walther P-5 9mm Parabellums.

"Four Walther P-5s," said Zulu as if in confirmation. "Three spare magazines for each pistol, magazines already loaded as are the ones in the pistols, and fifty extra rounds for anyone who needs them."

"No .45s, huh, or .357s?" a voice asked.

Zulu didn't turn to look, but said, "Major, the 9mm is usually adequate for killing people. And as you may know, the P-5, although rather new to the scene, is one of the best examples in the caliber. I'm sure you'll find it satisfactory, should the need arise."

"Oh, hey, I've fired them," Track was quick to add. "Great gun. I just like a little meatier caliber."

This time Zulu didn't answer. He simply continued removing a sheathed, black-handled knife from the case. "Four of these," he said, "Gerber Mark I fighting knives. The blade is a special type of stainless steel, I understand." Zulu turned toward Track. "Is a Gerber knife satisfactory, major?"

"Quite." Track smiled.

"Four of these as well, then. For the pistols, I have these." Zulu withdrew an object similar to an overly rotund knockwurst, but perhaps eight inches long. "We have a man who makes these for us. They're rather better than the Walther supersonic silencers or the various American or British makes. These pistols aren't fitted with slide locks, there wasn't any time. So if you can abide the mechanical noise, the silenced shots should sound like the proverbial 'phutt' of the spy films."

"I don't think I'm gonna like this," George volunteered.

"Really?" Zulu asked, looking over his shoulder at Beegh. "What a pity."

"Why four of everything?" Track asked the massive black man, but before Zulu could answer, Desiree interjected.

"I'm coming along to Abdul al-Kafir's with all of you," she said matter-of-factly.

"Bullshit," Track snapped.

"I'll second that," George added.

"I, too, had attempted to discourage Miss Desiree, but. . . ." Zulu turned his palms upward and shrugged. He returned to emptying the bottom of the huge suitcase.

Track looked at Desiree, but before he could say anything, she spoke.

"If you want my help in getting to see al-Kafir, I'm coming along." She smiled.

"If he's someone you can introduce me to, why all the guns and stuff?" demanded Track.

"He and I were never close. Al-Kafir's perversions disgusted me."

Track looked down at his hands, then at the hearth beside Zulu. "His perversions?" he asked.

Track felt Desiree's breath against his right cheek and right ear as she leaned to him, whispering. After a moment, he drew back and stared at her. "He does that?" he almost yelled, barely in control. "The slimy bastard."

"I'M BASIL OLAFSEN, room 304. I believe the desk rang that the package I was expecting had arrived?" Sergei Baslovitch lit a cigarette—this time a Player's—and waited. The hotel desk clerk smiled, turned away and took a small package from the shelf beneath the board of room keys. He appeared to study the address for an instant, then passed it over the desk. "Thank you," Baslovitch said in English. He was supposed to be a Swedish health-food salesman and unable to speak German.

"And thank you, Mein Herr," the clerk nodded deferentially.

Baslovitch weighed the package in his hands—it had to be the right article.

He walked across the foyer and down a hall toward a men's room he had seen, and pushed through the door with the package under his arm. Inside, he extracted a small pine wedge from his ski-jacket pocket and blocked the door closed with it. He sincerely hoped no one picked that instant for a case of diarrhea. He set the package on the steel shelf that ran under the mirror above the sinks. He ripped through the box because the adhesive tape was too resistant.

Inside the box was another box, this one wooden, closed with a tiny locked brass latch. Baslovitch took his key ring from his pocket and produced a tiny brass key. He unlocked the box.

Before him lay an H&K P-7 9mm, a squeeze cocker. Four 8-round magazines accompanied the gun, but there was no silencer. He felt inside the barrel with the top of his little finger. There was no threading for a silencer either. "Fuck-ups," he said in English.

The magazines were loaded, and he dropped them into his pocket. He checked the magazine in the pistol—it was loaded, too, and so was the chamber. Nine rounds there, plus thirty-two spares.

Baslovitch stuffed the empty cardboard box into a trash basket and stuck the slim, deadly pistol under his ski jacket in the elastic waistband of his slacks—he'd need a more secure spot. He washed his hands, studying his face in the mirror. Sometimes he thought seriously about defecting to the West. It wasn't politics. He believed in communism. It was just the way the KGB sometimes botched up things. He was worried that such inefficiency could be the death of him.

Baslovitch pocketed his wedge and left the men's

room. He started back toward the lobby. By now, his rented car should be waiting and with it his skis and other gear. As he passed the desk, he noticed the desk clerk watching him, then remembered he had the wooden box under his arm. Baslovitch smiled, again affecting his Swedish accent, and called out to the clerk as he walked past to the exit, "An old girlfriend knew I'd be staying here. Sent me a useful little good-luck charm."

## 8

The dark-haired girl's body writhed, her bare rear end twisting to the pounding drumbeat thumping out over the tape system. The twelve speakers, all perfectly balanced for bias shift, made the room pulse with sinister life. Abdul al-Kafir had balanced them himself, so he knew they were perfect. He could feel his palms sweat as he watched the girl from his glassed-in gallery, her barely postpubescent body rolling across the tiled floor beneath him.

He rubbed his palms on his thighs and raised his small swarthy left hand. He'd always had small hands. It had disturbed him as a boy, he remembered, watching his manicured left index finger as it pressed the red button.

The button emitted a buzzing sound, and he could see the girl's body tense, felt part of himself tense as he watched.

From where he sat, he could view the entire room. Drool began to drop from his lips as a gleaming stainless-steel door slid up into the upper wall and the glistening black bodies of three well-muscled Dobermans bounded in. The gleaming door closed.

He could see the tension in the girl's body as she became frozen with fear. He felt himself go rigid with anticipation.

Through the microphone feed he could hear her scream over the deep-throated growls of the Dobermans.

His left hand trembled as he turned up the volume.

The screaming grew louder.

The girl edged back toward the far wall on her right, slipped on her bare feet and fell spread-eagled.

The three Dobermans had stopped, watching her, their bodies quivering.

Abdul al-Kafir's body quivered with them.

He poised his left index finger over the green button. He was almost ready, his body trembling as he watched the dogs slowly advance on her.

She was screaming something incomprehensible in the dialect of his native tongue.

He liked white girls better—they screamed in English and screamed so much louder.

The girl was pleading, sobbing, as he lowered his finger on the green button.

Suddenly, he heard the pneumatic hiss of the door behind him as it opened.

Enraged, he moved his hand from the button and looked up.

Akhmed, his security chief, stood in the doorway.

"Get out of here!" al-Kafir screamed.

"But, master," pleaded Akhmed, his beady eyes shifting between al-Kafir and the scene in the room beyond the glass wall, "more than a score of commandos, heavily armed, approach the chalet from the mountainside on skis. And a car comes. I fear, master, fear that they come for you."

A part of Abdul al-Kafir went limp.

He stood quickly and zipped his pants, kicking over an eighteen-karat gold bowl with his left foot. "Allah curse them!" He felt his mouth twist into a snarl. "Kill the girl. But do not harm the dogs—to train them for this takes too long. See that the dogs are evacuated in the van. Immediately! And my car. It is ready?"

"Yes, master."

Abdul al-Kafir looked at the girl once more, heard her pleading. She was praying to him.

"About the killing of the girl—never mind that, Akhmed." Abdul al-Kafir pushed the green button. There was a buzzing sound different from the earlier noise and the three Dobermans lunged toward the girl, one for her face, one for her neck and one for her abdomen. She tried to twist away, but the drooling, white-fanged mouths of the dogs ripped into her flesh and began to tear her apart as if she were a rag doll.

Al-Kafir sighed, but the magic of the moment was ruined for him.

The screams died, and he saw a proud Doberman raise his blood-soaked head as he turned to leave the gallery.

AL-KAFIR PERSONALLY SUPERVISED the leading of the blood-splattered Dobermans into the special kennels in the dark-blue van. The attaché case he clutched against his chest contained the sum of his available cash outside his Swiss bank accounts—eighty-five thousand dollars in American currency—and his address book. The latter was worth more to him.

Akhmed—tall, dark, robust—exited the sprawling chalet and joined the three other members of the security force who surrounded al-Kafir as he started toward his vintage black Mercedes 600. Like the three others, Akhmed carried a Sterling submachine gun. Al-Kafir had first seen the reliability of British submachine guns in his dealings with the British before they had surrendered Palestine to the Jews in 1948. He had been twelve-years-old then, a panderer for the most profitable whorehouse in the Middle East and a Nazi sympathizer because of his hatred for the Jews.

Al-Kafir climbed into the rear seat of the Mercedes as Akhmed prepared to slam the door closed.

A car—another Mercedes—was coming up the road fast, skidding slightly on the hard-packed snow.

Al-Kafir's breath steamed in large clouds as he settled inside the cold car. Beside him, Akhmed shouted in English to the three German guards, "Stop that car—quickly!"

Al-Kafir hit the floor, feeling Akhmed shoving him down. He held his hands over his head. Gunfire roared, smashing through the plate-windows of the chalet. The chattering of submachine guns stuttered over the roar of the car's engine.

Suddenly the car wasn't moving. A short burst of submachine-gun fire was followed by a scream from one of the Germans.

He waited there, huddled on the floor of the car for what seemed a long time.

Finally he felt a hand on his shoulder.

He looked up into a broad black face, a huge man judging from the size of his hands.

"Would you join us, sir?" said a determined Zulu as he pulled a reluctant al-Kafir from the Mercedes with the grip of his right hand. An Uzi submachine gun, the muzzle pointed at al-Kafir's navel, was in his left.

Al-Kafir sagged back against the cold metal of his Mercedes and surveyed the scene.

He didn't like what he saw. Akhmed, hands raised in the air, stood beside the open cargo doors of the van housing the dogs. Inside, the animals were in a frenzy, throwing themselves against the doors of their cages. Two of the Germans were down in the snow. A river of red streamed from one of them. The other didn't have a head, and his blood was sprayed over the snow. The third German was on his knees in front of a big, young American-looking man. The American also held an Uzi. The German's left arm hung limp, a bloodied pulp from the elbow down.

A man with dark-brown hair and a dark mustache was walking toward the other Mercedes. He held a silenced pistol in his right hand. The collar of his brown leather bomber jacket was turned up against the cold, and his eyes were squinted against the glare of the sun. It looked as if he were somehow amused.

Then a woman stepped from the back seat of the second Mercedes, black leather gloves disappearing under the sleeves of an ermine midcalf-length coat. As she picked her way across the hard-packed snow of the driveway, a gust of wind caught at the coat, revealing an expensively tailored suit, the skirt just below the knee.

She removed sunglasses from her face with her gloved left hand and her blue eyes stared through him. The wind caught at her hair, and it shook like the mane of an Arabian stallion in its blackness and vibrance.

She, too, held a silenced pistol.

She spoke English perfectly—too perfectly to be natural, al-Kafir thought absently.

"Zulu, it was wise of you to visit our friend in Bludenze and borrow the Uzis for yourself and George."

"Thank you, Miss Desiree," the black man answered.

"Desiree? Desiree Goth?" Al-Kafir's jaw dropped.

"Abdul al-Kafir, what a thrill to meet you after so long," the woman smiled, making a limp-wristed gesture with the automatic in her right hand. "I think we've had mutual friends for years, haven't we? It's lovely, I think, for competitors to be able to meet so openly, on such an intimate basis."

"Yes, isn't it?" The man with the brown leather jacket laughed.

Desiree Goth approached al-Kafir, the wrist no longer limp. She raised the silenced pistol and stretched it toward his face. Al-Kafir felt himself swallow hard. "Miss Desiree," he faltered, "I—"

"Al-Kafir," she chided, her lips full, the voice a soft

alto. "You are the soul of the right-wing underground. We seek its most ardent devotee—one Johannes Krieger. He's stolen something all of us want for various reasons. Where can we find him?" The hammer of the automatic pistol cocked under her thumb. The muzzle didn't move.

"I do not know, Miss Desiree. His face is unknown to all—he is mystery, he is dangerous, too, this Krieger," pleaded al-Kafir.

"George?"

It was the man with the leather jacket who had spoken. Al-Kafir noticed the younger man with the pencil-thin mustache—turn around. "Yes, Uncle Dan?"

"Go over to al-Kafir. He's got a peculiar habit and he needs his hands to have fun with it. Start shooting off his fingers."

"Sure thing." George smiled. He shoved the German guard down into the snow, snapping, "Stay there," and then started across the driveway.

"Wait!" Al-Kafir had never heard such panic in his own voice.

"For what?" Desiree Goth smiled.

"Akhmed!" Al-Kafir shouted the name as shrilly as the girl had screamed for his mercy from the dogs, and immediately threw himself onto the snow beneath the level of Desiree Goth's pistol.

Akhmed had not been searched—at least Al-Kafir had not seen him being searched.

A sudden burst of blazing gunfire was answered by the muted sound of silenced weapons. As Al-Kafir rolled around the end of the Mercedes he heard the wild barking of the dogs and Akhmed's familiar voice, somehow strained, shouting, "Kill!"

SERGEI BASLOVITCH PEERED THROUGH the Zeiss armored binoculars, faintly amused. It was interesting to watch someone else working instead of himself. The Arab, al-Kafir, had thrown himself to the ground, shouting something that was incomprehensible at a distance. Baslovitch watched from the tree line, part way up a slope that ran at an oblique angle to the driveway leading to the chalet. He shuffled his feet in his Olins and watched. The big black man—his name was Zulu, the bodyguard of the gunrunner Desiree Goth—wheeled toward the Arab-looking man by the open cargo doors of the blue van. But the man with the full mustache and the leather jacket had moved first, firing a pistol. The Arab continued to fire what looked like a Beretta 92-SR in the auto mode. More gunfire cracked through the air and Baslovitch watched as the Arab with the Beretta pushed a fat al-Kafir through the side cargo doors of the van. He didn't see anyone fall.

Baslovitch settled his gaze on the man with the bomber jacket. He knew that face. It had haunted him since he'd first skied into the trees and broken out the binoculars, a face he hadn't seen since West Germany, a face from United States Army CID. "Major...hell, his name is Track!" He laughed. "Dan Track! I never forget a face," he mused.

Suddenly, there was a blur of blackness, then another. Baslovitch saw two dogs, Dobermans, large ones, spring onto the snow, their lips pulled back in vicious snarls, their man-killing teeth exposed and deadly. A younger-looking man, almost as big as the African Zulu, straight-armed one of the Dobermans in the chest, knocking it to the snow. A woman, Desiree Goth, fired a pistol, and the other dog took the shot in midair, twitching, lurching. Dan Track threw himself at the dying animal as it tried to lunge at Desiree Goth.

Track and the dog rolled in the snow, the wounded dog trying to force its teeth into Track's neck. A flash of steel glinted in the sunlight and Baslovitch heard a bellowing yelp from the dog and saw its muscled body go limp. Track rolled away from the magnificent dog of Satan, his knife and hand coated with blood.

The massive black man fired an Uzi, the recognizable profile of the weapon unmistakable. The other dog went down and didn't move.

The blue van was moving, and suddenly Baslovitch, taken up with enjoying the spectacle of the fight, realized al-Kafir and his tall Arab guard were gone.

The door of the van on the driver's side was slamming shut, the van already fishtailing as it skidded along the snowbank on the side of the driveway, sideswiping the Mercedes Dan Track and the others arrived in.

Involuntarily, Baslovitch recoiled, as a grenade or some other explosive device with similar force went off. The Mercedes lurched skyward, a fireball of orange and yellow and black belching around it.

Track and the younger man were running after the blue van. Zulu was helping Desiree Goth up from the snow, the back of her dark, midcalf-length fur coat white with the slick powder.

Above the dying roar of the explosion, Baslovitch heard a familiar chopping sound coming from above him.

A helicopter. He looked up and saw it. "Shit," was all he said.

He had secured the H&K P-7 9mm in an interior pocket of his ski jacket, and now it looked as if he'd be needing it. Baslovitch felt the corners of his mouth turn down in a frown. Either more of Desiree Goth's people had shown up, or a new player had sat down at the table. "At any rate," he said in English, "they're no friends of mine."

Baslovitch dug in his poles, letting the binoculars drop beneath his left armpit on their strap, and started cross-country after al-Kafir. There was still a job to be

done and that meant making al-Kafir talk about stolen
nuclear warheads.

MILES JEFFERSON SHOUTED to Ed Bartolinski, "Stop this
damn thing. The file says that blue van belongs to al-
Kafir!"

He threw open the door of the rented BMW and
stepped out on the passenger side, a Charter Arms two-
inch, six-shot stainless-steel .38 Special gripped tightly in
both his fists. The guns he had been given were a mixed
bag—a Colt Agent, a Smith & Wesson blue Chiefs Special and the Charter. He had taken the bobbed hammer,
stainless Charter because, of the three, it was the only one
designed to handle plus P.38 Special, like the two 158-
grain lead hollowpoint semiwadcutters he fired skyward
as the van bore down on them. It was stupid under the
conditions, but the driver's-side window was open and he
shouted it anyway. "Halt! Federal officers!"

The midnight-blue van kept coming.

"Shoot the fuckers!" shouted Jefferson's assistant,
David Palms.

Against his better judgment, but because it was the
only thing practical, Miles Jefferson shouted, "Palms,
take the tires. Bartolinski go for the radiator. I've got
the open driver's-side window!"

He swung the muzzle of the stainless Charter on line, firing, double actioning. It had a smooth trigger, he thought,
for a factory gun. He let loose two shots and the van swerv-
ed, two more, all six shots gone, the van's headlights were
shot out. The blue van wasn't stopping. Jefferson shrugged, maybe the tires were bullet-resistant.

He saw it as the driver tossed it. "Grenade!" he
yelled, and Jefferson launched himself over the
snowbank, out of the way, the little Charter in his right
hand, a Safariland speed-loader in his left.

He heard the explosion, his ears ringing with it, felt the concussion as it rippled over him, felt the snow pelting down on him.

He pushed himself up, ramming the speed-loader against the ejector star, greasing six more rounds into the Charter's cylinder. As he emptied the cylinder again against the rear doors of the fast vanishing blue van, he could see his hands—pink flesh in tiny shredded bits, flecked with blood.

Jefferson stepped back, stumbling in the snow and clambored over the snowbank. Ed Bartolinski was moving, getting to his feet, gasping, "I'm okay, I think." But David Palms would never move again—the whole left side of his body was ripped away, just like the roof and the hood of the BMW. Thick steaming splotches of dark-red blood and ragged chunks of pink flesh dotted the snow.

Jefferson wheeled, throwing up against the snowbank. Then coughing, half choking, he shouted after the van, "Son of a bitch!"

TRACK SKIDDED on the slick ice at the end of the driveway where it met the road. He'd emptied the Walther P-5, but hadn't stopped the van. And there had been another explosion perhaps a half mile down the road, just over the brow of the hill. Another grenade.

Overhead, the sounds of a helicopter filled the air with a staccato fury, and behind him, Desiree Goth screamed.

"Dan!"

Track slipped again as he spun around, caught his balance and started to run, ramming a fresh magazine up the butt of the Walther as he moved.

He could see George midway between him and Desiree, Zulu beside her. The wounded German guard was now sitting with his back propped against the side of al-Kafir's abandoned Mercedes.

Track was trying to figure out just whose helicopter was coming at them and what to do about it when ski-borne commandos, armed with assault rifles and sub-machine guns appeared from both sides of al-Kafir's chalet. The place was beginning to get crowded, Track thought to himself.

George was already firing toward them.

The Sikorsky was close, but Track couldn't look up and keep his balance on the ice-coated snow as he ran. "The chopper, George—the chopper!"

As if the occupants of the helicopter had heard him, knew the impending threat, machine-guns echoed fire overhead. Both sides of the snowpacked driveway on which Track ran were churning under the impact, and Track's hands came up to protect his face.

He could see Desiree through the storm of snow spit up by the machine-gun fire. Zulu was keeping her down beside the smoldering wreckage of the Mercedes, firing his Uzi skyward.

The ski troops—he counted twelve of them—were less than two hundred yards from the chalet, their assault rifles and subguns starting to spit fire.

"Dammit!" yelled Track as he dropped to his knees beside George. George fired his Uzi, and the snow around them churned as machine-gun fire rained down from the chopper as it made a second pass.

The Uzi belched neat 3-round bursts, while the Walther P-5 pumped in Track's hands. Their only chance was to disable the aircraft. He fired at the base of the main rotor blades, and at the rotor itself. He could see a crack starting in the bubble of the blue-and-white chopper as George's subgun fire tore into it.

Track counted two shots left in the Walther. The heli-copter was coming in low and fast, its machine guns sending out invitations to death. He triggered a single round from the Walther. There was an almost imperceptible difference in the chopper's movement. He fired the last round. With a sickening jerk, the rotor mechanism stopped. Like a giant bug, the chopper seemed to hang motionless in the air for a split second. Then it started to come down.

"George," Track yelled. "The snowbank—hit it!"

Track was moving fast, throwing himself over the snowbank, shouting to Desiree and Zulu, "She's comin' down. Take cover!"

His right shoulder hit the snowbank hard, his body taking the roll. His mouth filled with snow as he skidded down, and the ground began to shake under him as he heard the first sound wave, felt the first shock wave.

Bits of flaming debris rained down, and the snow was whipped into a skin-searing blizzard. Over the dying roar of the fatally wounded helicopter, Track heard something that sounded almost like a scream but barely human enough to be recognized as belonging to a man.

He rolled onto his back, his left hand protecting his eyes from the intense heat of the fireball that had erupted from the chopper's ruptured fuel tanks.

"Desiree!" He screamed her name. Up, running now, he rammed a fresh magazine into the P-5. The ski troops had taken cover beside the walls of the chalet, but they were moving again. Track could see that one of them was a woman.

Their automatic weapons opened up and hurled their deadly cargo into the devastating scene in front of the chalet.

"Desiree!" It was a loud whisper, like something from inside him rather than the sound of his own voice. She was moving, held tight against Zulu's hip as he fired toward the ski troops.

The snow beside Desiree and Zulu ripped up in a

wave, bursts of automatic-weapon fire hammered into
it. Track glanced to his right. George was still alive, had
survived the burning wreckage of the helicopter which
covered the width of the driveway. He was running, firing his Uzi with one hand, the Walther P-5 in the other.

Track was less than fifty yards from Desiree. She
turned and saw him, and he could see her eyes suddenly
widen. "Dan—save yourself!" she yelled.

"Bullshit!" He screamed the word, his throat aching
with it.

Twenty-five yards. Twenty. Zulu was running, leaving Desiree for an instant by the far side of their Mercedes. The massive black man drew fire as he rolled
across the snow toward the end of the driveway. Then
he was up on his feet, his Uzi firing out messages that
were stamped "No return, please." Zulu ran, diving
into the snow near the far edge of the driveway. Track
narrowed the distance to Desiree to ten yards.

Zulu shouted, "Major—here!"

Track wheeled half-right, pumping the Walther's trigger twice, dropping a man with an M-16 as he skied
down toward Zulu. Zulu sailed one of the Sterling subguns toward him, and Track stabbed the Walther into
his waistband and caught it. He found the safety by feel
and swung the muzzle on line toward the ski troops, firing. He could see George diving for a snowbank.

Track dodged left, toward Desiree crouched beside
the wrecked Mercedes. She was firing her silenced P-5.
"Get down, dammit, Desiree," Track rasped as he skidded across the snow and dropped beside her.

He pushed her down hard as he rammed the muzzle
of the Sterling over what remained of the Mercedes's
trunk and started to fire. Two men went down, a line of
red splotches patterning their white commando suits. A
third spun headless into the snowbank near Zulu.

"Dan!"

It was George.

"More of them coming up!" he yelled.

Track twisted around, trying to guess how many shots remained in the Sterling's 34-round stick. He had no idea how many had already been fired when he'd gotten the weapon from Zulu.

At the far end of the driveway, where it met the road, he could see two men running beyond the smoldering ruins of the helicopter.

He started to raise the Sterling, then held the muzzle down. The tall black man was Miles Jefferson. He remembered having seen the man with him, but couldn't place the name.

"The FBI—all we need," Track yelled to Desiree.

"Here?" she asked incredulously.

"Don't ask me, this isn't my scenario." He turned back to prod the muzzle of the Sterling over the Mercedes. Heavy assault rifle and subgun fire ripped into the steel of the scorched and twisted trunk lid. He pumped the Sterling's trigger, two 3-round bursts, dropping one more member of the ski troops.

The Sterling was empty.

"Shit," stormed Track, and he threw the gun aside. He tore Desiree's Walther from her hands and yanked his own from his waistband. "Keep your head down!" He fired both pistols, one in each fist, shouting to George, "Those guys are FBI—Miles Jefferson, remember?"

"Here?" screeched George.

"Same thing Desiree said," Track shouted back across the snowpacked driveway. Then he turned toward the wreckage of the helicopter. Jefferson and the other FBI man were crouched beside the mangled tail section. "Miles! The bad guys are the ones on skis. Stay back!" Track shouted.

He didn't wait for an answer. There were at least ten

of the ski troops still moving; there must have been more of them than he had originally seen. They slalomed along the sides of the slopes, firing their weapons with each pass.

George and Zulu stood shoulder to shoulder, two huge men fighting for more than just their lives. Their Uzi subguns were jumping in their hands, and three more of the ski troopers went down.

Track heard a woman's voice shouting something in German, but he couldn't make it out. The skiers changed their pattern of movement, forming a wedge, and started down the slope on the far side of the driveway, their weapons blazing death.

"Did you hear what she said?" asked Desiree.

"I couldn't make it out," Track said as he rammed a fresh magazine into the Walther.

"Something like...forget them...we want al-Kafir. Something like that."

"Keep your head down, now!" Track lurched against her, shoving her down, shielding her with his body. Seven skiers were coming fast, shooting up over George and Zulu's position. The wedge broke toward the twisted Mercedes.

Gunfire echoed and reechoed from the body of the Mercedes as Track covered Desiree with his body.

He dropped one of the skiers, but six slipped away across the drop of the slope paralleling the driveway and sped toward the road. "They're out to get al-Kafir, dammit!" Track exclaimed. He was up, hauling Desiree to her feet. "Got those spare magazines in your purse?" he said holding out his hand.

"My three? Yes," she said.

"Good—give them to me." He stood beside her for an instant, then added, "Get them from you in a minute." He ran across the driveway and pulled back the mask on a dead skier. German, possibly. Definitely

European. Who, he wondered, had sent them? They were well trained, and their equipment was first-rate. They must have been dropped higher on the slope by the helicopter.

Track glanced down at the dead skier's boots. The foot size was too small.

He ran toward the snowbank and yelled to Zulu and George, "Find me a body with size twelve or so boots, hurry!"

He crossed the snowbank and checked another body. This one was a younger man, about George's age, Track guessed, and he too looked to be German. Again, the boots were too small.

"Here, Dan!" It was George, and Track ran toward him. "His gunboats look as big as yours."

They were Raichle's, the ski boots with the flexible tongue. He began stripping them from the dead man, George helping.

Behind him, he could hear Miles Jefferson. "What the hell is goin' on here, Track?"

"Not FBI business, so don't push it, Miles, or you'll be all over the front page of Pravda. American imperialist secret police invade Austria—shit like that."

"What are you doing?" Jefferson continued.

Still without looking, Track starting to strip off his Italian Vasque hiking boots. Sitting in the snow, he told Miles, "I've got to stop that scum in the blue van."

"Abdul al-Kafir?" Jefferson remarked, raising his eyebrow slightly.

"Yeah," growled Track, "got to get him—probably want him for the same reason you want him."

"On skis," questioned Jefferson, "you're gonna catch him on skis?"

"You drove up the same way we did probably," Track told the man. "Past Kandahar. Now al-Kafir's going to have to go around it. But it looks like there's a side trail there," said Track, pointing along the mountain, "that would intersect the road."

"You're crazy, man—" retorted Jefferson.

"Do you ski?" asked Track. "Are you volunteering to go—or is your car just down the road?"

"The bastard blew up our car," Jefferson snapped. "And I don't ski."

"Yeah, well, I used to a lot. I hope it's like swimming and riding a bicycle," said Track.

Track stood up. George had set out the skis and was finding a set of poles. Track stepped into the bindings and locked them. The skis were Heads. Desiree was picking her way across the slick, iced-over snow, and Track watched her for an instant.

As he did he could hear Zulu's voice. "Major, I have a submachine gun here and three spare magazines."

Track looked at the bodyguard. "Fine, but I'll rely on the pistol and use this only as a backup. I'm not good enough to ski with both hands involved." He took the Sterling and slung it cross body from left shoulder to right hip. George handed him a small blue teardrop rucksack. "Thanks," Track nodded, slinging it on his back. He could feel Zulu behind him, securing the magazines inside.

Desiree stopped less than a yard from him. "You don't have to do this," she said.

"Yeah, I know. That's why I'm doin' it. Say I have to do something and I usually won't."

"Then you have to do this," she said, her face expressionless.

He reached out to her, kissed her quickly, felt her body yield against his for an instant. "Now, those spare magazines of yours," was all he could trust his voice to say.

Her eyes flickered as she handed him three fresh magazines for the Walther P-5.

Track stuffed the spare mags into his pants pockets, checked out his own Walther and shoved it into his waistband.

"What the hell you doin' with a silenced pistol, Track?" Miles Jefferson interrupted.

Before Track could answer, Zulu said, "Sir, because we are both relatively close racially, please don't labor under the misapprehension I wouldn't shoot your knee-caps should that become necessary."

George laughed.

Track felt Zulu's hands at the backpack again. "More Walther magazines—I had two extras. They're yours now."

"Thanks, but I still don't like you," Track said with a grin.

"The feeling is ever mutual, major." That was Zulu. Cuddly as ever.

Track shot a grin at the big black man. "Take care of our baby, huh?"

There was something like the flicker of a smile in Zulu's almost-black eyes. "As always, major, as always. And please don't get killed. I was rather looking forward to that pleasure myself some day."

"Do my best," Track nodded. He looked into Desiree's eyes. "I know—be reckless." He stabbed his poles into the snow. They weren't quite the right height but they'd do. He shouted, "Meet you in the village. Have a nice walk."

He didn't really think they'd walk. There was likely another car in the garage under the base of the chalet. But cross-country was the only way to catch Abdul al-Kafir and the blue van—maybe.

## 9

Baslovitch dug in with the inside edge of his downhill ski and brought himself to a stop. The blue van was still roughly parallel to him but more than a mile away on the road beneath him. He started to move again, but caught himself. On one of the more remote slopes of the Kandahar he saw movement, like a man in motion down the slope. Dangling his poles from his wrists, he snatched up the Zeiss binoculars, smudging condensation from the lenses, and swung them to the Kandahar. It was one of the finest slopes in the world. He focused on the man. The leather jacket was brown, the height seemed right.

"Track," he growled. Baslovitch watched his adversary for a moment, studying his technique. From the ease with which Track handled himself, the body flex in the turns, which he used to control his speed, Baslovitch guessed that he'd learned to ski by the Graduated Length Method. Baslovitch had learned in the traditional way and still used the stem a great deal.

It was clear what Track was doing—making up for lost time by taking the faster, more dangerous slope in an effort to intersect the road and get ahead of the fleeing van. It was a good strategy, and Track was roughly parallel to him now.

"Very good, my friend," Baslovitch remarked as he watched through the binoculars. "But for your sake, I hope you are not too good—or I'll have to kill you. A promise." Baslovitch let the binoculars fall to his side and grabbed at the handles of his poles again, digging in, bending his body low as he attacked the slope.

He would need greater speed now, in order to beat Track and intercept the blue van first. His body bent forward over the tips of his skis and he threw himself into the downhill, fast and dangerous.

TRACK USED BODY ENGLISH to slow himself as he moved into the turn, skidding a little on the edge of his ski, his poles digging in.

It was coming back to him. He hadn't skied since Europe had been his beat for Army CID.

On the road a thousand yards beneath him, he could see the dark form of the speeding van. The only way to beat the Arab to the point of the road beneath this side trail of Kandahar, he thought, would be to run it all out. And somewhere ahead of him—somewhere, though he couldn't see them—were six of the heavily armed ski troops. One of them, the apparent leader, was a woman.

If everyone from Desiree Goth to the FBI was coming to Abdul al-Kafir for information on Johannes Krieger, Track surmised the ski troops were representing Krieger, sent to eliminate al-Kafir as a possible source of betrayal.

"What the hell," he rasped into the wind, and he knifed his body into the downhill run. At the speed he was building to, a fall could mean a broken back or neck—likely death, and that would be preferable to the alternatives.

The frigid air around him was numbing now, carrying with it the buffeting of the wind. His body danced on his skis for balance, his knees flexed, the poles tucked up under his armpits. If the Walther pistol in his waistband were to begin to come loose, he'd have to leave it, to let it go and be lost. A sudden shift in balance would be disaster now, he knew.

Track could no longer feel the pain of the wind and cold against his face. With his hips over his skis, he swung his shoulders fast, working his ankles and veering right around a mogul, flexing back, bending into the slope. The blue van was barely visible through the blizzard of ice and snow whipped up by the wind.

His lips drawn back, Track felt his teeth bared. He sucked his breath against the cold, trying to warm the air in his mouth before taking it into his lungs. The trail split ahead of him. To the left ran a gentler slope, but Track could see now that it curved along the side of the mountain and would take him perhaps a mile out of his way.

To the right, the trail was steeper, sharper. A sign posted in German warned him off his chosen path. Ten feet beyond it another sign, this one in bold orange letters, simply read, *Gefahr*. It was German for danger.

"No shit," Track snarled into the wind, taking the path to his right. Another sign read Halt! It meant the same in German as it did in English, but it was too late now for Track to stop. And then he saw why the signs had been posted. A quarter mile ahead, the trail swept up suddenly and beyond it was nothing but blue sky.

He worked his body English, turning himself, nearly losing it. Regaining his balance, he slowed and stopped, amazed that he could actually do that.

Ahead, beyond the drop-off, he could see airspace, and perhaps a hundred feet beyond it, virgin snow. There was no telling if the lip of the trail was solid or merely formed from blowing and drifting snow.

If it was solid, considering the distance down, he could try for a jump and hope to make it across.

"If," he murmured.

He could no longer see the road, and herringboning it back to where the two trails had diverged would take forever.

He looked behind him, then ahead.

It was reckless. It was stupid. But if al-Kafir died before he gave up whatever it was he knew about Johannes Krieger, then perhaps the 500-kiloton warheads would be lost. Perhaps Krieger was even now preparing to detonate one, to kill millions of innocent people, he thought.

Track closed his eyes for an instant, Desiree's face in his thoughts. He wanted to return to her, to be with her, awake and asleep.

But despite her joke, there was no other world where she could go to escape the nuclear devastation the ninety-nine remaining warheads could wreak.

He shrugged and arched his eyebrows. "Oh, well...." If the lip of the trail was only of snow, or if the gap between one side of the small saddle back and the other was too wide he hoped he would die quickly and not have to endure the agony of freezing to death with every bone in his body broken.

He dug in his poles and kicked off trying to focus his thoughts on making the jump. He had about four hundred yards to work up speed. His legs ached, his neck ached. He then tried focusing onto something else: How many bones were there in the human body anyway? Two hundred six? Was that right?

The lip of the trail was coming, and Track's direction suddenly changed. The trail was like a ramp now and his body was low as he rocketed upward, steeper and steeper.

He could feel the edge of the lip giving way, but he was already launched into the air, his shoulders hunched, his head down, his poles up, his knees flexed for the impact. He was falling, but still traveling forward. Below him were snow-splotched rocks. He focused his eyes ahead. The edge of the far side of the saddle was farther away than he had thought. He tucked

up, then angled his body forward over the tips of his
skis, trying to push the last millimeter of distance from
the jump.

His rate of descent was too fast. He thought he would
fall below the edge of the far side of the saddle before he
had traveled far enough outward. He arched his back,
leaning at a sharp angle, almost flat across his skis now.

He felt the impact, and his body vibrated with it. His
legs wavered dangerously, his balance shifting radically.

Finally, he got his balance and redistributed his
weight. He crouched his body into a tuck, going faster
on the skis than he had ever gone before.

"Yahoo!" He screamed the word so loud his throat
ached, his lungs suddenly cold with the intake of air.

But he kept going.

The trail curved as it gently banked downhill. From his
uphill position, Track could see the midnight-blue van of
al-Kafir again. The van had more than a mile to travel
before it reached the segment of road beneath the trail.

Track leaned over his skis, tucked up his poles, and
turned into the curve. Now he was heading straight
down. One mistake and he'd be dead. In the distance,
he could see a single dark-clad shape racing down the
opposite slope.

It wasn't one of the ski troopers, unless whoever it
was had thrown away his snow smock.

It was someone new.

"Didn't know we were having a party," he said to
himself.

The trail zigzagged left, a massive mogul at its ap-
proximate center. Track leaned to the trail's right embankment, spiked his poles into the snow, and launched
himself over the mogul. The Sterling submachine gun
rocked against his right side, and the pressure of the
Walther P-5 with its silencer against his abdomen made
him wince.

The figure on the opposite slope was in sharper definition. From the general build and the way the person handled the skis he assumed it was a man. He was a classic European skier, putting every ounce of energy into it.

Track felt his lips curl in a smile against the wind. He wondered who it was.

There was no assault rifle in evidence, and the distance was too great to see a submachine gun that might be slung across the back.

Track skied the rim of the embankment again and bounced over another mogul. He came down hard and fast and maneuvered his way into balance again. The trail was almost at an end, the road coming up fast.

To his right he saw the van, and he could almost make out the figure behind the windshield.

There was apparently a third trail, one he hadn't seen, for two hundred yards behind the blue van, he could see the half-dozen ski troopers in hot pursuit.

The van fishtailed as it picked up speed. Assault rifle and subgun fire cracked out behind the van, coming from the advancing ski troopers. Across the road, coming down the far slope, he could see the mysterious skier. Both of his poles had been transferred to his left hand, and in the right the shape of a pistol jutted forth.

With the speed at which he traveled, Track judged that he and the lone skier would intersect the road at approximately the same instant, and at approximately the same spot, from opposite sides. They would be between the van and the six ski troopers.

"Shit!" he shouted. A gunfight on skis wasn't what he wanted.

Track shifted both poles to his left hand and dug in. He pulled the Sterling up on its sling and charged the chamber with the top cartridge from the 34-round magazine. He worked the bolt, and set the safety on. Everything was ready for a firefight. Track grasped his poles again with his left hand, and coasted forward.

The trail started upward, toward the embankment of snow that flanked the road. Track let the Sterling fall to his side on its sling and shifted one pole back to his right hand.

He looked up to see the lone skier airborne, sailing over the far embankment.

Track dug in his poles, twisting his body, digging his poles into the snow and ice of the road.

Beside him, less than ten feet away, was the lone skier. The pistol in the man's right hand was a Heckler & Koch P-7. He couldn't make out the face, twisted against the stinging wind, half shrouded by a knit headband, the goggles protecting the eyes.

Track shifted his right pole to his left hand again. The Sterling slipped forward, and his thumb worked off the safety. Gunfire began to stutter from behind him.

He glanced toward the mysterious skier, a tall, lean, well-muscled man.

The man was looking at him.

Their eyes met through their goggles.

Track thought he saw a smile as the man twisted his balance on his skis and fired a 2-round semiauto burst from the little H&K toward the ski troopers.

Track glanced behind him once and saw one of the troopers going down.

Track shouted to the man beside him, "All right, let's nail those bastards and settle between us later."

"That sounds good to me," the shout came back in unaccented English.

Track let the Sterling swing across his chest. Taking his poles in both hands, he dug in and executed a 180-degree turn. He came down hard and pushed himself backward down the road after the receding van. It would be seconds before he lost momentum or hit a rut.

Both poles dangled from his wrists as he brought the Sterling up and fired, burning out the magazine toward the five remaining ski troopers. He killed three, and blood sprayed out from their bodies over the snow. The third man spun out spectacularly over the embankment, then disappeared from sight.

Assault-rifle fire continued from the remaining two. They were good skiers, balancing themselves only with their weapons.

Track let the emptied Sterling fall on its sling and stabbed his poles into the ice-slicked snow of the road, twisting, losing his balance, starting to fall. Suddenly the solo skier was beside him, supporting him for an instant. Track regained his balance, nodded to the man and shouted over the roar of gunfire from behind and the laboring engine noises of the blue van fifty yards ahead, "I'm all right!"

The man nodded, twisted on his skis and fired the little pistol again, spending the magazine. A shout from the skier, "Missed!"

As the solo skier changed magazines for the little 9mm, Track reached under his leather bomber jacket. His fingers closed around the butt of the Walther P-5, and he jerked it free of his waistband. Track fired over his left shoulder, once, twice, a third time. One of the ski troopers took a shot in the left arm and his assault rifle fell to the snow. But the skier was still coming, and as Track looked back again, he saw that the lost assault rifle had been replaced by a revolver. A .357, Track guessed as the echo of the first shot rang in his ears.

Track pumped the Walther's trigger two more times, but missed.

He turned away, digging his poles in with his left hand.

"Together—together we can get them!"

It was the lone skier shouting to him.

Track glanced to the man and nodded as he zigzagged on his skis to avoid the assault-rifle fire from the woman ski trooper. Gunfire tracked along the road surface and cutting waves of ice chips pelted up at him.

Track found the P-5's magazine release and changed to one of the fresh ammo sticks in his jacket pocket. He rammed it up the butt—nine shots now.

"Ready?" Track shouted to the other man.

"Ready, comrade!" came the reply.

Track raised his eyebrows and stared at the man. The voice—and the expression. He had heard that voice once before, years ago when he was still a captain in the CID, before his promotion to major, before leaving the Army.

"Baslovitch?" he said aloud.

"You have a wonderful memory, Major Track!" Baslovitch looked away, then back toward Track. "Truce until we stop them?"

Track nodded to the KGB man. They had fought before, to a draw. "Truce—until we stop them," Track echoed.

"My count of three. One, two...." Track readied the silenced Walther P-5. "Three!"

Track twisted right, pumping the P-5's trigger behind him, toward the man with the revolver, the cough-cough sounds of his own pistol punctuated by the sharp cracks of Baslovitch's 9mm. The man with the revolver went down, sprawling backward into the snow. Baslovitch's target was the woman and Track watched as the Russian's slugs ripped into her. Her assault rifle flew from her hands and she clasped at her chest, before snapping out her arms. With her body momentarily frozen in the shape of a cross she veered left and up the embankment, sprawling over it, out of sight.

Track twisted forward, struggling to keep his balance.

"We did it!" Baslovitch shouted, skiing closer, then

suddenly reaching out. "The truce is over, Major Track!"

Track felt the impact, the butt of the pistol hammering against the left side of his neck. He felt his balance going. He was falling, cursing Baslovitch as the Russian rocketed ahead.

Track sprawled onto the road surface. His bindings sprung open, and his left ski slithered down the road ahead of him.

Track spread-eagled his arms and legs to slow his spinning skid across the ice-slicked snow. He raised his head to see Baslovitch taking the left embankment, in an attempt to cut off al-Kafir's van. Track raised his pistol. He had one shot left as he touched the P-5's trigger, aiming for Baslovitch's rear end—he had no desire to kill the man. But Baslovitch was airborne, going over the embankment of snow and ice. As the Walther bucked in his hands, Track saw the left ski twist away and split in half. Baslovitch was airborne for one instant, then gone from sight with a shout of rage.

Track rammed a fresh magazine up the butt of the pistol, dropped the hammer, and pushed the Walther back into his waistband. As he retrieved his ski, his only thought was to catch the blue van and al-Kafir. And the only way to intercept the van was to try the same stunt Baslovitch had tried.

As he picked up speed, he lowered his body over his skis and looked for the best spot to shoot over the embankment. He saw it, and dug in his poles.

As Track shot up the embankment he could hear Baslovitch behind him, cursing, "Bastard! You rotten bastard!"

But unless Baslovitch was good at changing magazines on the fly and in midair, his pistol wouldn't be loaded. At least Track hoped it wouldn't.

Ahead, there was another embankment as the road

made a hairpin curve. Track sideslipped a mogul, gaining speed. The wind had chiseled the top of the embankment flat and Track launched himself forward toward it.

He was roughly parallel to the van now and could see the burly Arab behind the wheel. Al-Kafir, he thought, must still be in the back.

Al-Kafir's driver had seen him and raised a pistol to fire. Track realized he had no time to get to his P-5. As the Arab swung his gun out of the driver's-side window, Track freed his wrist from the strap and held his right pole at the balance point. Track hurtled it with all his might toward the driver. The pole whistled through the open window and burrowed into the driver's head slightly forward and above his left ear. The big Arab slumped over the wheel. The van went into a sudden zigzag, and Track could hear al-Kafir screaming for help from the back.

Track felt his lips twist into a grin. "Asshole," he snarled. The van hammered repeatedly against the embankment, and Track could hear al-Kafir moaning as he bounced around the inside.

Suddenly, the van caught a rut and angled sharply, away from the embankment toward the far side of the road. Track could see the ground drop off to a precipice ahead. The van would go over the side, and al-Kafir would be killed. "Jump for it!" Track shouted.

Al-Kafir's whining bleat in the cold air made him somehow nauseated. "I can't. I'm afraid!"

Track could see the angle of the van and the edge of the road. In less than a minute, perhaps much less, the van would be over the side.

Track hurled himself toward the van, praying the impact would break away his bindings before he broke his ankles or his legs.

He slammed down hard on the roof of the careering

vehicle, his skis gone. He could feel his body starting to roll off the roof of the runaway van.

Summoning all of his force, he stabbed his remaining ski pole downward into the roof of the van.

His right hand reached for the pole and grabbed at it, as his left hand slid across the roof line and his fingers locked over the opening for the driver's window.

The pole snapped with a crack, and Track's body lurched to the right. As he started to slide from the roof, his right hand made a desperate grab for the window opening on the passenger side.

He was falling. His hands clutched at the opening, and his feet dragged in the snow. Pain shot up his back but if he let go he knew al-Kafir would die and take whatever information he had on Johannes Krieger to the grave with him.

Track felt the muscles in his arms extend; his neck was tight with pain. With his jaw set, he tugged himself forward, his left hand reaching for the door handle.

He had it, and the door swung open, Track's body swinging with it. His feet ripped a furrow in the snow. He could hear the open-door warning buzzer sounding from the dashboard as he swung his right foot up and wedged it against the interior of the door. The door slapped closed, pressing his body between door and doorframe. His right hand stabbed out for the steering wheel, which was jammed beneath the deadweight of the driver.

The lip of the road was less than fifty yards away. Track had to gamble. He threw his body forward and across the seat. If he fell now he would go under the wheels.

He could hear al-Kafir screaming from the back of the van. Another sound made his blood run cold. A third Doberman was still in the van, and the door of his cage must have rattled loose from all the shaking.

Track pulled the body of the dead driver aside, and twisted in behind the wheel. In the rearview mirror he could see past the hinged Plexiglas sheet that separated the driver's compartment from the rear of the van. A huge dark shape lunged at al-Kafir.

The van went into a slide, and Track fought the wheel into the skid.

He could see over the edge of the road—perhaps six feet and then nothing.

Inside his gloves his hands sweated.

The Doberman continued his ferocious assault on al-Kafir and Track winced at the thought of the damage such an animal could inflict.

He started pumping the brake, first pressure, then no presure, again and again.

As the snarls of the Doberman merged with al-Kafir's desperate cries for help, Track increased the brake pressure. Gradually, the van slowed. The rear end danced to the right, coming within feet of the soft precipice.

Finally, it came to a stop.

Track heard a throttled cry and looked back into the cargo bay of the van. The Doberman's huge mouth seemed to cover al-Kafir's entire face, tearing at his throat. Al-Kafir's blood flowed freely, and as Track watched, the fat Arab's hands dropped from the dog's neck. He saw a glint of steel as al-Kafir came up with a sleek, thin dagger in a last desperate attempt to save his life. The blade swept upward and plunged into the Doberman's stomach.

The big black dog let out a piercing yelp and whipped its head to the side, tearing away half of al-Kafir's throat with its sudden movement. The big animal's back legs jerked in spasms, slipping in the pool of blood that gushed from al-Kafir's neck. The Arab's chubby hand still gripped the jeweled handle of the dagger as the dog collapsed on him.

Track pushed open the Plexiglas divider and stared into the cargo area. The hot blood steamed as cold air swept through the van. Al-Kafir was propped against the inside of the van, his eyes bulging grotesquely from his face. Track could see the exposed vertebrae of his neck where the Doberman had ripped his way through muscle and tendon. The dog's blood-covered snout lay across al-Kafir's chest.

Nothing moved.

Finally, Track summoned up the strength to crawl into the back of the van. He winced as he banged his head hard on the roof. There was a puncture hole in the interior of the roof from the ski pole, and Track shivered thinking about how close he came to being dead too.

A briefcase lay on the floor, the lock secured. Track took the Gerber knife from under his jacket and pried at the lockplate. It resisted.

He shrugged, using the knife instead to cut through the leather.

Inside was American money—a lot of it, in fifties and hundreds. He decided he'd determine its fate later.

Under the money was an address book.

He opened it and saw what appeared to be phone numbers. But there were no names attached. Track figured that if they were important enough to be in code, they were important enough to read.

He looked at the lifeless al-Kafir, the man who Desiree Goth had said enjoyed watching young girls being ripped apart by dogs.

He felt that some sort of justice had prevailed.

He didn't try to feel sorry.

## 10

"I wasn't in Air Force Intelligence for nothing," George laughed, poring over al-Kafir's address book. Desiree sat on the edge of George's chair, while Track leaned against the mantle, Zulu beisde him. Track's borrowed P-5 was cleaned and reloaded. Zulu had the Uzi tucked under an opened copy of a Zurich newspaper. Al-Kafir might have friends in the area, and there was always the possibility that Baslovitch would come calling—also with friends.

George spoke again. "Actually, we didn't do anything with codes like this, but I sort of got into it as a hobby. I had a friend who loved working anagrams and puzzles—and I think I know what this is. Unplug the telephone and bring it over here, Uncle Dan."

"Gotcha, George," Track replied, shifting his weight off the mantle. As he walked across the room, he started to feel stiff. He needed a hot shower but he needed the lead first and hoped al-Kafir's book would provide it.

He reached down to the wall and noticed the telephone wasn't the modular kind and didn't unplug. He shrugged. He wasn't expecting any calls anyway. He ripped the cord from the wall and brought the phone to the table by the window where George and Desiree sat.

"What do you want with this," Track asked.

"Save me trying to remember the dial. You ripped it out of the wall?" George laughed, looking at the frayed cord and then at Track.

"When I'm tired I do stuff like that, and I'm tired,"

Track replied. He found one of his cigars and started to bite off the tip. "Anybody mind if I smoke one of these—and I mean besides you?" He turned and grinned at Zulu.

Desiree chuckled. "After what you did? If I'd done it, even I'd smoke one."

Track nodded, sitting down opposite Desiree and George, squinting against the light. His eyes stung from fatigue.

"Okay," George began. "This is a very basic kind of code and so obvious it's the sort of thing you could put a computer on and blow out a fuse with it."

Zulu walked over to the table, and stared down. Track looked away from him, lighting the cigar. "Whip it on me, George," Track told his nephew.

"All right. First, the telephone dial. The number 1 doesn't have any letters with it, and the letter 0 at the other end isn't really a letter at all. It's really a zero, and there aren't any letters with it either. So, you look at these phone numbers and count the number 1 and the 0 as placeholders. Positioners if you like."

"I like," Track said with a laugh. "What the hell are you talking about?"

"A very basic code I believe, major," Zulu observed.

"Right," George grinned. He lighted a Winston, then looked back at the address book. "Okay. He has a phone number in here—area code 217, then 660-5031. I don't think it's anyone's phone number. I think it spells out Arnold."

Desiree piped up. "Arnold Tosch is a member of the right-wing underground. He's an assassin."

"Here's how it works," George continued. "The first letter of Arnold is A, and that corresponds to the number 2 on the dial or touch tone. But with the A there's also B and C."

"So how do you know which one is which," Track interrupted.

The placeholders or identifiers, like I said. In 217, the 2 shows which hole in the dial or which key on a touch tone, the 1 shows us which position the letter is in. If it had been Ackroyd instead of Arnold, it would have been 207 instead of 217, because the 0 would signify to use the last letter of the triad. If the name were Abner instead of Arnold, he wouldn't have used a 1 or an 0— just moved on to the next key for the next letter.''

"So a ten digit phone number spells out Arnold?"

"Right, Dan, and this next number is—" George peered at the book, "Yeah, here, area code 816 and the number is 070-2044, a fake prefix if I ever heard one. The repetition of the number 4 is just doubling the letter H at the end of Arnold Tosch. Al-Kafir probably has addresses the same way and other information, too, all like phone numbers. So all I've got to do is translate all these phone numbers, and we can work a decoding of the whole book—everything.''

"I shall borrow some additional telephones, then we can share your burden," Zulu proclaimed. Track didn't even want to know how Zulu planned to do it.

An hour later, they had come up with a detailed reference to Joannes Krieger. Apparently, Krieger could be contacted through a woman known as Marlena Fields. No further translation had been necessary after that, though eventually the entire book would be worked out, picked clean of useful information and anonymously dropped on the CIA.

Marlena Fields was known to Desiree Goth as a political assassin and right-wing terrorist.

Zulu had started down to the hotel lobby to use a working telephone, but returned after only a moment. "Those gentlemen from the FBI, I think they wish to converse with us," Zulu announced, reentering the room.

Track, who'd been lying across the bed, his eyes still sore, opened them. "Any local authorities with them?"

"My first thought, major. Apparently not, however."

"George, in the bathroom with an Uzi—quick!" Track ordered, as he picked up the silenced P-5 from the nightstand and slid it under the pillow.

There was a knock at the door. Zulu's eyes flickered toward Track. Track nodded, turning on his side, his right hand near the pillow.

He listened, watching.

Zulu opened the door. "Yes—ahh—our American law enforcement friends from the snowfields!"

Track started to laugh, hearing Miles Jefferson but not seeing him yet.

"Look, you jive son of a bitch. You left me and Bartolinski out there near al-Kafir's house to freeze to death, or whatever, while you and that dame and Track's nephew took the only car that wasn't blown up and drove away like bats outta hell. Where's Dan Track?"

"In here, Miles," Track sang out. He gave Desiree a wink and she smiled back at him. She was pretty, he thought, more than pretty.

Zulu stepped aside, and Miles Jefferson and the other FBI man stalked through the doorway. Jefferson blurted out, "If this were stateside all of you'd be in the slammer for everything from assaulting an officer, to murder, to the Mann Act."

"Mann Act? Doesn't that involve underage girls." Desiree smiled, sitting at the table beside the window, a book open on her lap. "I'm flattered, Agent Jefferson, but I'm not underage."

"I didn't mean you, lady. I meant what we found left of some poor kid in al-Kafir's chalet."

"Al-Kafir is dead," Track told Jefferson matter-of-factly.

"Yeah," nodded Jefferson, "we found the van.

Shouldn't keep pets if you can't take care of them. But what about Johannes Krieger," Jefferson insisted, advancing across the room.

"When I get something concrete you'll get it, too. I wish I could expect the same from you, Miles," Track replied without conviction.

"I want you and this insurance cartel and this lady gunrunner and her Limey bodyguard and that nephew of yours outta my hair. This is government business," ordered Jefferson.

"Or what?" Desiree Goth purred. Track craned his neck again to look at her. "Just what does the government want with Johannes Krieger?"

"You know damn well what we want, lady. And from what I know about you, you want the same thing we do, but to sell 'em." Miles was feeling rude.

"Ohh," smiled Desiree, "those warheads. Yes, that would be nice."

"So back off," Jefferson shouted. "Just damn well back off, 'cause if the law here in Austria can't touch you, I'll touch you, all of you, so help me. I'm tired, cold, angry, and I got the President of the United States breathing down my neck for those warheads."

Track lowered his voice to a whisper, saying, "Sorry about Palms getting killed. He was okay. Would you like a drink?"

Jefferson stabbed his hands into his pockets, looked down at the floor for an instant and then at Track. "No, I already had one. Where the hell's that George Beegh, your nephew?"

Track let himself grin. "Taking a crap, if you'll excuse the expression."

"Dan," Miles Jefferson began. "There was a briefcase loaded with money in al-Kafir's van. If you didn't take the money, you took something else. I want it—evidence."

"Nothing you'd be interested in," Track advised.

"Right," and Jefferson's right hand flashed under his coat and reappeared with a snub-nosed shiny revolver. "Now, let me ask that question again."

Track raised his voice a little, watching as the second FBI man drew his firearm. "You think walking in here with a gun is going to get you what you want, Miles...."

Track didn't get a chance to finish. The bathroom door burst open, and George blazed through, dropped to one knee and covered the room with the Uzi. "Raise those hands—fast, guys," George said with a smile. "I think I forgot to flush."

"Aw, shit," Jefferson growled.

George grinned. "How'd you know?"

## 11

The first of the two phone calls was the one Track considered the most important, he had told George. "Yeah, Tassles, it's me, sweetheart. How's things?...great— yeah...yeah, I miss Dorothy, too."

"Dorothy?" Zulu asked, bending closer to George in the office borrowed from the Consortium.

"Dorothy the Wonder Cat," George told him.

"Dorothy the Wonder Cat," repeated Zulu, shaking his head. "Major Track is, as I feared, insane."

George laughed at that. "Maybe, but Dorothy's important to him."

"And Tassles, is that another cat?" Zulu continued.

"No," replied George, "that's Tassles LaToure the famous stripper, Dan's secretary."

"Ahh, a wonder cat and a striptease dancer, how interesting," and Zulu stood up, walked across the small office and stared out through the venetian blind. George hadn't looked much at the Athens street scenes. After some time in Greece with the air force, he had already seen quite a bit of it.

He tuned back in to his uncle's conversation. "FBI guys, huh? Well, tell them to contact me in Greece.... No, don't tell them where in Greece, just say Greece.... Gotcha, sweetheart—would I ever, huh?" Track laughed. "Nobody does it like you do, kid," and he hung up.

George felt a smile creep onto his face as Desiree Goth asked, "And who is Dorothy's baby-sitter, this Tassles LaToure you mentioned?"

"George went out with her, I don't. She's more George's type, honest, kid," said Track with a mischievous grin.

George closed his eyes. Someday, he promised himself, he'd get even with his uncle. "Uncle Dan set me up with a date with Tassles, never told me she was sixty-three, though." George opened his eyes then closed them again. Desiree Goth looked as if she was holding back a smile.

The phone rang, and George opened his eyes, watching his uncle. "Yeah, put him through.... Sir Abner? Dan, here...yeah...yeah, some trouble. With the cops. I need you to—" There was a long pause. Track's face looked ashen, George thought. "A what?" Track nodded into the phone. "Wait a minute." Then he cupped his palm over the receiver. "Miles Jefferson tracked us to Greece. He's got the Greek government out after me, just me. Some kind of warrant for attempted murder," Track whispered to the room.

"Attempted murder!" George repeated. "All we did was take his clothes and his gun and all the drapes off the windows and covers off the bed and lock him and the other guy in your hotel room when we left Austria."

Zulu laughed.

"Well, you know," Track grinned. "Some guys get pissed off at little things." Track shrugged and turned back to the phone. "Yeah, I figured it was something like that. You've got to get the heat off me. Desiree thinks she's got something on this Marlena Fields that can lead us to her, maybe then to Krieger. I can't sit around in the Athens slammer just because Miles Jefferson's got a hard-on for my scalp.... Right...I know...but work a miracle anyway and then get here to Athens right away because we're going to need you and the gear...I know...I know that, too...but I'd rather have my own stuff.... Yeah...I'll leave word with the office here where you can find me. . . . Good idea so we don't get the local Consortium guy here in trouble— sealed envelope addressed to you. . . . Right. . . all right. See you soon, and do what you can to call off Miles, huh? Right. Bye-bye,'' and Track hung up.

Track looked at George, then at Desiree, then at Zulu. "Sir Abner should be able to get that warrant, or whatever it is, killed, but it'll take at least a day. And if some cop spots my face, I'm—"

"I should know in an hour," Desiree interrupted, "on which island Marlena Fields makes her headquarters. And Zulu and I can smuggle you out of the country. We have considerable experience, you'll just have to accept that on faith."

George watched his uncle start to laugh. He lit a cigarette. It wasn't funny to him at all.

His own gear had not yet arrived and Track, carrying another Walther P-5 and an Uzi submachine gun provided by Desiree Goth from another of her mysterious sources, waited by the gunwales of the old fishing boat. He felt slightly theatrical, dressed all in black—a long-sleeved knit shirt, the front buttoned nearly to the neck, and black slacks and black crepe-soled shoes. He looked at George, dressed identically, standing beside him. The blackness of Zulu's clothing seemed to accentuate the blackness of his skin, and made him appear almost like a shadow.

Desiree, as she did in any clothes, seemed exquisite.

Track had insisted that she not come, and she had insisted that she would not reveal the location of the island, nor secure weapons for him if she did not. He backed down. She was, he told himself, a grown-up woman, had a right to make her own decisions and risk her own neck. Somehow, the rationalization hadn't eased his fears for her safety.

He, George and Zulu had been smuggled out of Athens in caskets, with Desiree disguising herself as a Greek widow lamenting the death of her husband and two brothers in a fiery accident. Once, when the truck had slowed, Track had thought they had been found out, but then the truck had picked up speed again.

The truck had carried them to an airfield, and by amphibious aircraft, they had flown down through the Aegean toward Crete, not going quite that far.

The plane had landed on water and they quickly transferred to a fishing boat. It was a smuggling vessel owned by Desiree, with nothing outwardly visible that could distinguish it from the other vessels that plied the seas. But in secret compartments built into the bowels of the ship were sophisticated radar gear, radio systems, sonar devices and weapons closets.

Track, George, Zulu and Desiree weren't alone on the deck as the dark island gradually became more defined.

With them stood twelve men, similarly clad and armed. Business associates of Desiree's.

Track slid his arm about her waist and whispered to her in the darkness, "What are you proving by coming along?"

"I don't have to prove anything," she answered. "I'm coming because I wish to come."

"Awful gritty business maybe. And these night clothes are hardly fashionable," he said, laughing softly.

He felt her breath on his ear as she leaned up and whispered beside his left cheek, "But I'm wearing silk underwear with handmade lace. I'll survive it."

Track held her against him. On the island would be Marlena Fields and perhaps as many as fifty right-wing terrorists—Nazis, Turkish Grey Wolves, the lot. And maybe—Track swallowed hard as he thought of it—just maybe Johannes Krieger.

The throb of the engines stopped beneath his feet.

Desiree's voice beside him startled him. *"Pameh! Pameh!"* she ordered.

Her Greek sounded perfect, as it had since they had first departed the plane in Athens on a flight from Zurich. And she had told her men, ordered them, "Let's go!"

A man wearing four knives, at least that was how many were visible, did a handspring over the rail into the launch, and started to work at the pulleys to run it down from the davits into the water.

*"Ghreegorah!"* It was Desiree again. And hurry the crew did.

HE STROKED AT HIS BEARD. That everyone knew it was not a real beard didn't bother him much. He wore it as though it were one. He sat by the yellow lamplight, just listening. The high collared navy-blue turtleneck kept him comfortably warm against the cold breeze blowing in from the ocean. He smoked a cigarette, an American brand, Chesterfield. One of Marlena's men smuggled cigarettes. Compulsively, Johannes Krieger switched brands to match his role.

He thought about the news from Austria.

Johannes Krieger didn't like failure.

He watched Marlena Fields. She was addressing a group of men and women who stood around the walls of the room. The room itself was at the top of the tower of the monastery that dominated the center of the island.

"It is imperative that all of you when you leave tonight realize the ultimate importance of his task," she intoned. "The destruction of the existing world order and its replacement with the one true order."

That she spoke in English to these men and women seemed natural enough to Krieger. They were of mixed nationalities. Most of them were Turks, but there were also some Greeks, some Germans, some Austrians, and two Frenchmen. English, however well or poorly it was understood by those assembled at the edge of the lamplight, was the only common bond, besides a belief in the principles of National Socialism and the destiny of mankind.

Krieger sat aloof at the opposite end of the partially roofless structure. There would be another night of sleep with Marlena, another night of being the subject of her desire. At first it had pleased him but now it was wearisome.

"Tonight, the seaplanes shall come and each of you shall be taken to the points for your individual missions," Marlena continued. "Tonight, you link hands with destiny," this last phrase she almost whispered.

Marlena Fields then turned to Johannes Krieger. There was wildness in her eyes that bespoke savagery, a headier lust than she showed even in bed. "Johannes," she cried, "a word for our warriors of the Reich."

Krieger nodded and stood, inhaling on his cigarette. He smiled. It was one of the moments that would be written in the history books. Perhaps some of these books would recount it as part of the legend.

As Krieger spoke, he established eye contact with each of them for a brief instant. "We stand at the threshold of destiny, which the very evolution of mankind has ordained that only we can fulfill." He felt badly speaking this way before Greek and Turks. Their racial heritage was so mixed. "Each task, however small it may seem, is of vital importance in the framework of our plan. Not all of you will even see one of the warheads, and some of you will not live to tell of this hour to your children and your children's children. But we strike the blow, the fatal blow, which is at once the breath of life and the wind of change. Go forth assured in the knowledge that you are about the business of destiny. And may the spirit of our dead leader live again through you, see again through your eyes, triumph through your deeds.'' He raised his right hand in the classic salute he had learned as a boy. Heels snapped together as the others raised their right hands as well.

Krieger was slightly amused at himself for becoming emotional. His throat felt a momentary tightness and he sniffed loudly to hold back a tear.

"Destiny," he whispered. The lamplight flickered. It had flickered throughout much of the evening of talk, of dreams. But it did not die out.

## 12

Dan Track shielded Desiree Goth with his left arm, the
Walther pistol clenched tight in his right fist as he
looked skyward. The clouds parted briefly in the
growing wind and shafts of moonlight illuminated the
sea and sky. He could hear and then see a second
plane.

Whatever was on the island, he thought as a third aircraft came into view, the planes were part of it.

"George, take five men around to the right, find a
path that parallels this one and hang back a little to
cover us if we bump into something."

Then his eyes searched out Zulu's black face. "Krieger is important," he said, "but not as important as
someone else."

"Perhaps someday I shall like you, major," conceded
Zulu, "but in the distant future—and should we both
live that long, of course."

"Did you actually say something nice to me?" Track
asked.

"I certainly hope not, major, but I shall remain at
Miss Desiree's side."

Track nodded, not knowing if Zulu could see him. He
started forward, feeling Desiree close behind him. He
wished he'd listened more closely at the tactics classes
he'd attended in Officer's Candidacy School. Instead he
was banking on common sense and logic. And luck. If
he were Marlena Fields or Johannes Krieger and guarding the small island, this is the way he would place sen-

tries. He hoped he was right, and he reached out for the top of a rough pillar of rock.

As if on cue, the clouds broke as Track peered across the flat top of the rock. The brightness of a full moon bathed the landscape before him. His left hand gave the silencer on the Walther a good-luck twist as he stared across the central part of the island. Towering columns of rock, silhouetted against the sky, dominated the terrain. They provided a natural fortification. High on a flat promontory, rose a flat-topped mountain of rock. Perched upon it was a collection of half-ruined walls and buildings. He knew that on the far side of the mesa was a course down to the sea. Another aircraft flew overhead. It was dropping in altitude, and in the brightness of the moonlight, he could see pontoons beneath the fuselage. A seaplane.

He turned to Desiree. "Looks like either fresh personnel coming in or whoever's here going out," he said.

"It is well to remember," Zulu murmured, "that the fishing boat may have been seen from the air. Our arrival may be at least partially anticipated."

"Good thought, but I hope you're wrong," Track nodded in the darkness. "We'll keep working our way toward the ruins, link up with George and his men and play it by ear." He looked at the rest of the men. "If you don't understand my English well enough, I'll have Desiree translate into Greek—but keep it as quiet as you can. Don't bunch together. No shooting unless you have to. If there's a sentry that needs putting away, use knives or garrotes. If you have to shoot, use a weapon with a silencer. The less notice they have that we're coming, the better off we'll be and the less distance we'll have to cover once the fighting starts. So, any questions? Everyone understand?"

Everyone did.

He shrugged, turned away from the seven crewmen

and started ahead. The blanket of cloud folded back to cover the moon.

GEORGE BEEGH, a Walther P-5 in his right hand, tucked down into the shadow of the rocks. Two men stood less than fifty yards away, their bodies and their weapons, submachine guns, profiled against the dull light diffused through the cloud cover. The moon had just disappeared. For the few moments it had been wholly visible, George had thought that reaching the two sentries would be impossible.

He signaled to the Greek called Xanthos, who was beside him. The smuggler gestured toward the two men, then silently withdrew his knife.

George looked at the glint of steel, then nodded. But he held out his left hand to restrain Xanthos for a moment. Using hand signals, George told the other four men to wait. He holstered the P-5, the silencer protruding through the bottom.

He withdrew the Gerber Mark I fighting knife from the sheath lashed to the inside of the calf of his left leg. Gesturing to Xanthos, George started forward. He had been in fights and battles—but he had never before crept up on a stranger to knife him to death.

He let Xanthos move slightly ahead, to observe the man's technique. From the way the knife seemed to mold to Xanthos' hand, it was evident that the blade had seen much use.

George knew the classic techniques. Approach from the rear and dig the thumb and forefinger into the eye sockets and draw the head back to expose the neck, simultaneously ripping the blade across the throat to cut the voice box and stifle any cry. Or, cover the mouth with the left hand and hammer the knife hand forward into the right kidney. There were a lot of ways to kill, all of them more preferable to being killed.

His palms sweated inside the gloves. He clenched the knife between his teeth, careful of the edge closest to the corners of his mouth lest he draw his own blood.

He moved ahead, in a low, fast crouch, knowing what he would do now if he could.

Xanthos stopped, paused, then sprang forward like a jungle cat attacking from the shadows. He was on the guard to the right, pouncing, the knife vanishing from sight.

The other man turned and raised his submachine gun.

George hurtled himself forward, his left fist hammering out across the subgunner's jaw. He heard the sound of teeth breaking. The guard fell back, and George hit him with a left backhand. The man, stumbling, started to turn on him. His body rocked as George's left fist connected, followed by a right to the middle of his face. George could feel the nose crush under his knuckles.

The subgunner's body crumpled to the dirt.

George fell upon him, ready with the knife, but he didn't need to use it. The smashed nose had apparently punched upward into the brain. The man was undeniably dead. As the clouds split and moonlight suddenly bathed the ground, a large moth landed on the subgunner's open right eye, then flew away. The eye never blinked.

George sagged over the man for an instant, almost feeling sorry for him. "Shit," he whispered, the knife still in his teeth.

He looked at Xanthos, as the Greek cleaned his knife on the clothes of the other dead sentry. *"Thraxos!"* the Greek smuggler grinned as he pointed to George. It was the Greek word for courage.

George picked up the weapons of his victim—an Uzi submachine gun, a commando knife and one of the little, inexpensive German revolvers. From the diameter of the hole at the muzzle George guessed it was a .22 caliber.

Discarding the knife and the subgun, for which there was only one magazine, George pocketed the revolver and started to drag off the body.

The target was the ruined monastery at the center of the island. Towers of rock formed a natural wall on three sides of it.

Before attacking the sentries, he had seen lights in the monastery, one a dimly glowing yellow light.

Overhead, there was the sound of another aircraft.

"Oh, boy," he groaned.

He dumped the body, then kept going with Xanthos and the others.

AHEAD OF HIM, Track could make out three sentries, armed with submachine guns. With Zulu and one of the Greek smugglers from Desiree's crew, whose name was Adrianos, Track moved toward the three men through the darkness. Immediately beyond them was the nearest of the pillars of rock, and beyond that the ruined monastery.

Track held a garrote in his hands, three feet of piano wire with wooden pegs at each end. He held it ready to loop.

Zulu was bare-handed.

Track reflected that if he were Zulu's size, he could take out an armed sentry bare-handed as well.

Track kept moving, timing himself with Zulu and Adrianos.

He stopped, waiting in the shadows. The three guards were talking in heavily accented English.

"That Krieger—he is a strange one I think," said the tallest of the three.

Another voice added, "First he is a Greek religious man," the accent French, "and now that beard and the wig. I wonder if Marlena knows his face when she sleeps with him."

A third guard, this one short and stocky, spoke up in an accent that was hard to define and heavy. "You betcha she knows somethin' else, you betcha. She sleeps with Krieger every night. Whatever he got she knows it good."

"Ha," the tall one laughed.

The stocky guard spoke again. "The assignment you were given, where do you go from here?"

"We are not supposed to tell of this," the Frenchman answered. "But to Paris—there is one of the bombs there, I think."

"Warheads," the man who dwarfed his cohorts corrected. "But we use like bombs." And he laughed.

Track started forward, flanked by Zulu and Adrianos.

Suddenly Track stopped. One of the men who had been sitting on a rock started to stand, and standing would make him face the direction from which Track and the others came.

It was now or never.

Track focused his concentration on the garrote and not the man to avoid some sixth sense the man might have to warn himself. He ran forward, the garrote ready, just as the one with the French accent, Track's target of the three, turned around.

Track launched himself toward the man and, in one quick motion, looped the garrote over his throat. There was the beginning of a cry as Track twisted his own body hard left, hauling the Frenchman's body up over his right shoulder by the garrote. He felt the weight, then suddenly the weight was slipping away, the garrote free.

Track didn't turn to look. The man's head was severed and Track didn't have to see it. He could hear the man's hot blood spill out onto the cool rocks.

He threw himself toward the second of the three sentries, who was locked in combat with the Greek smuggler. Adrianos went down, his knife clattering to the rocks, and the sentry raised his submachine gun to fire.

Track's body hurled into the sentry, and he hauled the man down. The heel of his left hand hammered out and up, against the base of the sentry's nose, driving it up through the bone and into the brain.

The third man, Zulu's target, was on the ground. The bizarre angle of the head indicated that death had come swiftly and suddenly with a broken neck.

Track snapped his fingers once, the signal for Desiree to come forward.

She rushed to his arms. "Are you all right, Dan?" Her voice was a low whisper in the darkness.

"Things have been better," he whispered back. "I'd rather be in bed, actually."

He saw that she was looking behind him, her blue eyes wide in the half light. "I never...."

"A man with his head cut off—right," and he turned her away, letting her fall against Zulu. He stared toward the monastery beyond the pillars of rock, then dropped into a crouch in the shadows, signaling the others to do the same.

"There could be more sentries anywhere among these rock pillars," he whispered. "Stupid for all of us to go on together."

Track looked hard at Zulu. "Stay with Desiree and run things here," he said. "Give me a five-minute start." Track glanced at the luminous black face of his watch. "In five minutes I'll meet you at the entrance to the monastery. You, Adrianos," he said as he turned to look at the Greek who had had difficulty with the second sentry. "Take off at a right angle and intercept my nephew, but be careful they recognize you. Go with him and cover the back door of the monastery. Shoot anyone that comes out that way unless it's one of us. If George feels you can, start to penetrate the monastery from that end. Got a watch?''

Adrianos nodded.

"Good. Tell George to start the attack at eleven-fifteen, unless he needs to sooner. Now move out and *kalee tehee*, huh?" said Track.

"And good luck to you, sir," Adrianos said with a grin, evidently pleased at the responsibility he'd been given after botching the sentry removal.

Track looked at Desiree. "Think warm thoughts, kid," he said. Taking back his Uzi from one of Desiree's men, Track started into the darkness between the nearest of the stone pillars.

TRACK DISCOVERED JUST ONE SENTRY in the area between the pillars of rock and the base of the mesa that supported the monastery. Track removed him permanently with the little Gerber Mark I, plunging it into the carotid artery while he suffocated the man until the blood loss caused unconsciousness.

Track ran as silently as he could on the gravel and dirt surface, toward a bank of rough-hewn stone steps that edged their way up the perpendicular side of the mesa. Evidently they were carved by the original inhabitants of the monastery hundreds of years before.

His body hugged the wall of the mesa and he took the narrow, treacherous steps one at a time.

Suddenly, he froze. Footsteps shuffled on the steps ahead of him, and he sniffed the acrid smell of cigarette smoke.

His eyes flickered to the silenced 9mm autoloader in his gloved right hand. He rammed the pistol into his trouser band under his knit shirt, suddenly feeling the coldness of the night.

If it were one man, and it sounded like only one, fine,

he thought. If there were two or more, what he planned would be fatal.

Track squeezed himself even further into the rock and waited.

The footsteps grew louder, the smell of cigarette smoke stronger. A tall, well-muscled man, a cigarette cupped in his right hand, was on top of him almost before he realized. Track's right fist slammed out into the man's Adam's apple and crushed the windpipe. But he felt his knuckles deflect as the man's head instinctively recoiled.

Track's right knee smashed up for the groin, glanced off the metal of a submachine gun, and hammered the man in the crotch with almost full force.

As the man doubled forward, Track's left crossed his jaw and he went down heavily.

Track caught the body as it started to slip away, and dragged the unconscious man beside the wall. Track reached for the Gerber knife, ready to use it to silence the man permanently.

He hesitated. "Dumb ass softie," he snarled to himself.

Track put away the knife, and quickly searched the man. He pocketed a cheap Japanese lockblade folding knife that opened like a switchblade, and took a spare magazine slung across the man's abdomen.

He took the Uzi as well. What the hell.

In the man's right front pocket was a handkerchief. Track pulled it out, and stuffed it into the man's mouth. He ripped the victim's belt from his blue jeans and bound his ankles. He reached down to the track shoes, pulled out one of the laces and used it to secure the gag.

He worked out the second shoelace, and whipped it around the man's wrists, binding them. It might be just as well to take a few prisoners, Track reasoned. They might be able to tell him a few things about Johannes Krieger and the missing warheads.

   With two Uzis swung across his body, his own and the
one from the unconscious and bound terrorist, he
started up the stone steps again, the silenced Walther
back in his right fist.

## 13

Krieger looked at Marlena Fields, her face close to his chest, her breath hot on his skin. The warmth of the covers made him feel lazy, tired.

*"Ich liebe Dich, Johannes,"* she whispered to him

"Love me?" he replied. "Whatever would you love me for?"

"You are brave, strong—you are kind to me in bed. It is something I feel, Johannes."

He reached over to the upturned crate beside the bed and found his cigarettes. He lit one with a butane lighter, inhaling the smoke deeply. "You are sweet to say those things to me," he finally told her. "But until this is all over, darling, we both know...." He let the rest of his thoughts hang on the cool air around them.

He glanced at the Omega wristwatch he wore in his current persona. It was nearly eleven-fifteen. "All the planes will be landed soon, one more should be coming in. I need to get going now."

"But..." she stammered.

"The pilots will need their briefings and they must adhere to their departure schedules," he said.

"Can't we once more, then—quickly, please?"

With his fingertips, he began to stroke her already-aroused nipples. She moaned softly, whispering, "After this, with the Soviet fighter and Gurnheim's work in America, when can we...?"

"If Klaus had prepared the Russian device so that it is truly foolproof, it will be the first step. The final step

will come soon," he told her. "Perhaps then. But there
will be much work for us both, Marlena."

He rolled over on her, and slipped between her
already-sticky thighs. He felt himself get erect in her
hands and quickly entered her. She whispered, "Your
face, I must see it, must know it!" And before he could
stop her, her hands flashed upward and he felt the tearing of his flesh as she ripped at the beard glued to his
face and tore away the wig, the tape ripping at his own
hair.

"Johannes," she gasped.

He fell forward against her, his hands closing about
her throat. With what he felt was actually sincerity, he
whispered to her as he closed his hands, "I'm sorry darling—*auf wiedersehen*, Marlena."

Johannes Krieger's thumbs pressed over her larynx,
crushing it as she coughed the words, "I love you."

The false beard was ripped irreparably, and he stood
naked in the cold darkness of the room, trying to think.
The briefing of the pilots had to be made before the men
and women assembled to board the seaplanes could over-
hear his instructions. His instructions were simple but
vital. "In the event of detection, bail out and crash the
plane into the sea." The sound of his own voice in the
stillness shocked him.

He walked back to the bed, and sat down. What little
moonlight came through the partially shuttered window
reflected from Marlena's open eyes. He thumbed them
closed.

## 14

With Adrianos beside him and five more men on the other side of the rear opening into the rock-walled monastery, George stood and waited, straddling the body of a dead sentry Adrianos had killed with a knife.

He glanced down at his Rolex. It was nearly eleven-fifteen and yet there had been no sounds of battle, no gunfire from inside the monastery walls or beyond on the far side where his uncle and the others would make their approach.

At eleven-fifteen he was supposed to attack, two minutes from now.

"Adrianos," George barked. "Take two men with you, that one and that one," and he gestured toward them. "The other three come with me. We go through as fire-and-maneuver elements. We'll start in and you cover us. When we get a position, I'll signal if I can; otherwise just guess at it that we're ready to cover for you and advance. Stick to opposite sides of the corridors, so there's less chance of a grenade or a machine gun pinning all of us down. Understand?" He didn't mean to be rude to Adrianos. The man seemed capable enough, with the important exception of a solid knowledge of English.

"Fire and maneuver, yes. Understand good, you are ready?" Adrianos said with a grin.

George nodded and licked his lips. He reached under his black knit shirt, found the bill of his Jack Daniels baseball cap and pulled it on.

"Now I'm ready," he told Adrianos. He glanced at the Rolex. Eleven-fifteen. "Give 'em hell!" he shouted, and he started through the entranceway, firing a burst from his Uzi.

"Atta boy, George," Track hissed under his breath. He glanced at his Rolex. They had synchronized watches and George was dead-on time. He regretted the phrasing of the thought. There had to be a better word than dead. He started to run and got nearly to the top of the winding stone steps.

He stopped at eye level with the base of the arched opening through the monastery wall. Men and women were running away from him, toward the rear entrance of the walled grounds. Gunfire was visible in bright flashes from the far side of the wall, and submachine guns and assault rifles started to return fire from inside the monastery compound.

Track raised his pistol as a man ran past the steps, not looking toward him. He was firing a burst of assault-rifle fire toward the muzzle flashes from George and his men. Track rammed the pistol up and against the man's rib cage, stepping up the last three steps in one stride as he moved. He fired the Walther twice, and the body fell away. Track worked the decocking lever and grabbed up the assault rifle.

The rifle was an M-16, stolen from some overseas armory he guessed. He kept the selector on full auto and ran across the compound, firing at targets of opportunity, putting the terrorists down with even 3-round bursts until the assault rifle was empty.

A man charged at him from the shadows of the wall and Track snapped the butt of the M-16 into the center of the man's face. He felt the facial bones collapse beneath the blow and the man sunk away.

He threw down the empty M-16, shifted one of the

two Uzis forward on its sling, and continued to run.

If Krieger were there, he would be inside the monastery building itself. And if not, at least Marlena Fields would be there. And she would have the information he needed. Track could feel it inside him.

Either way, he had to penetrate the monastery building.

Track pumped the Uzi's trigger as he ran through the shadows.

"MARLENA, WHAT SHOULD WE DO?" shouted one of the men from below the gallery overlooking the ground floor.

"Fight to the death if you must," came the voice from above, "as many of you as possible must reach the planes. Kill the invaders. Johannes Krieger has charged us with this duty!"

"To the death," a Frenchman shouted. But Johannes Krieger reflected that Frenchmen were always slightly on the dramatic side. It was part of the national heritage, he supposed. He stepped back from the balcony, swathed in Marlena's robe and a shawl. He had her voice down perfectly. It was something he unconsciously did with people, learning to imitate them. Unfortunately, it was as far as the impersonation could go for the moment, and he turned from the mezzanine overlooking the chapel and ran back down the hallway, bursting through the curtained doorway and into the room he had shared with Marlena.

There was no way to repair the bearded image he had affected before. The torn wig was all but ruined. Hurriedly, he threw off the shawl that covered his hair and his face, and started for the battered dresser, that Marlena had used for some of her things. He hoped she had a wig.

For a moment, he caught sight of his own face in the

mirror. The high cheekbones and abrupt, demanding jawline only drew attention to the eyes, which burned with ferocity.

It was a face he rarely saw.

He removed his contact lenses and decided to use his own eye color as part of a disguise. He dropped the green lenses to the stone floor and crushed them under the heel of his white track shoes.

Marlena would have makeup, but only the simple things a woman used. Aside from too much lipstick, she wore little makeup—had worn little makeup, he corrected.

He turned and glanced at her naked body on the bed. He felt nothing.

He looked back to the top drawer of the dresser, but found only underwear and a cachet of fragrance. He slammed the drawer shut, and continued through the second drawer, then the one beneath it.

"Aha!" he exclaimed. He removed the garments, and held up to view a loose-looking red-velour jogging outfit, with a high neckline and knitted cuffs, waistband and ankles. It would fit with the track shoes.

From the drawer above he took a bra and then took more of the underwear to use as padding for a fake bustline.

"Hair," he muttered. He returned to Marlena's body and roughly rolled her over. He caught up her hair from the nape of the neck. With a shawl, the hair could be used to construct the appearance of real hair beneath it. Marlena's eye color was close to his.

"It will work," he said confidently. He took a switch-blade from the hip pocket of his jeans and hacked the hair from the back of her head.

He still had the gum he had used to secure the beard, and there was more wigtape.

Quickly, he stripped away his own clothing.

He kept his legs and chest shaved smooth, and set about crafting the disguise. He expected that the assault force in the monastery courtyard, whatever its composition, would wait approximately ten minutes before penetrating the interior of the monastery.

That would be time enough for a fast change of identities and escape with the help of Marlena's loyal personnel. And when Marlena's body was found, total confusion would overtake his enemies.

"Confusion to my enemies," he laughed, carefully starting to dress.

He studied his image in the mirror. The makeup had appeared to lower his cheekbones and lightened his skin tones. With the shawl in place, what little of the spirit-gummed hair that was visible seemed to show Marlena's hair in slight disarray, as would be expected.

He stepped back from the mirror.

The red jogging suit was unfashionably tight but satisfactory.

He grabbed Marlena's purse, taking money, identification and other useful items in quick inventory, then cached his own few possessions inside it as well.

He would leave his pistol behind. There wasn't room for it in the purse. Instead, he took Marlena's SIG-Sauer P-226 double column magazine 9mm.

She had spare magazines. He left these in the purse.

He started for the doorway, and gave a last look to Marlena on the bed. The gunfire raged outside and below.

"I look better as you than you did, darling," he said, laughing, then stepped through the curtained doorway. The voice with which he had spoken was her voice.

And now she was he.

KRIEGER PICKED HIS WAY down a wooden staircase in the semi-darkness. A fire burned in the courtyard where an incendiary device had ignited the gasoline that fuelled the generator system. The beacon on the far side of the monastery needed electric lights for guiding the seaplanes to their landing spot.

It was this side of the monastery to which he now ran.

To his left he heard a voice. "Marlena, the power boat is ready for you, and one of the pilots awaits with his engine running. We can get you to safety."

Krieger turned around, his face swathed with the scarf. In Marlena's voice, he answered, "*Sehr gut*, Franz—then we must hurry. And the men?"

"They fight well, but some of the attackers have entered the monastery. We must use the hidden staircase to the sea."

"Hidden staircase?" Krieger repeated in a muffled whisper. His thoughts turned to Marlena and he felt himself smile. She had held out one secret from him after all. A hidden escape route. He wondered how many other secrets went to the grave with her.

"Lead the way, Franz," he answered in Marlena's voice. Franz ran past him, and gave him a gentle love pat on his left shoulder.

Keeping his knees closer together than he normally would have and kicking out his heels, Krieger ran. Marlena's run, he thought.

For an instant, as he followed Franz around a twist in the corridor and up a narrow ramp, he wondered if somewhere along the way he had lost sight completely of his own identity. He had not been Johannes Krieger for so long he wondered if he felt more natural in someone else's life, with someone else's visage.

He ran on, the passage taking a turn, the ramp turning sharply downward.

And faintly, very faintly as he ran, he could smell the sea and feel the cold air blowing in off the water.

He smiled again. He knew that victory waited out there for him to lay his claim.

The word "insane" flitted across his mind, but he dismissed it.

TRACK HAD BOXED HIMSELF in just inside the entrance to the monastery itself. Heavy fire from assault rifles and submachine guns came at him like hail from a portico cut into the wall beneath a balcony-like mezzanine that hung over what had obviously been a chapel at one time.

It was a holding action, Track realized, and an effective one.

Gunfire thundered out behind him, and Track wheeled on his knees toward it, one of the Uzis up and ready. If there were such a thing as sixth sense, it had just saved him from killing his own nephew, he realized. George, two of the Greek smugglers, and behind them Desiree and Zulu raced through the doorway and into the chapel. Their submachine guns blazed fire and death.

Track shouted a warning to them across the stone room, "Here—look out for the portico under the mezzanine!" Track turned his own weapon toward the portico and fired out a 32-round magazine, diverting attention from his friends. Then he rammed a fresh one up the well in the pistol grip.

He glanced left. George and Zulu and one of the Greeks sprayed out a covering fire as Desiree and the other Greek ran toward Track's position, Desiree wing-shooting her pistol.

The Greek took a burst in his midsection, and Desiree cut her sprint, dropped to her knees and fired her silenced P-5 toward the portico. As she edged toward the Greek, Track leaped up and started toward her. He fired his Uzi one-handed, then swung the second Uzi forward and pumped its trigger as well.

She fired out her Walther and quickly picked up the fallen Greek's Uzi, tugging to free the sling from the man's arm. A fusilade of automatic-weapons fire poured from the portico under the balcony, sending stone chips flying from the floor like shrapnel.

Track dropped to his knees, still in motion and slid across the floor toward her. He pushed her down and shielded her body with his own, as he fired both Uzis simultaneously toward the portico. He stole a glance at the man beside Desiree. He was dead.

Track shouted to Zulu and George. "Come on, I've got Desiree!" Letting one of the Uzis drop to his side on its sling, Track rammed a fresh 32-round stick up the magazine well. He protracted the stock, and with the metal butt half against his right hip bone as he braced the weapon, he let loose a fusilade of shots. Desiree was on her feet, firing the Uzi that the dead man had carried. Together, they blasted their way to safety.

Track brought her down beside a flight of low steps on the far right hand side of the entrance, and pushed her against the stone. He polked the muzzle of his Uzi over the treads of the stone steps, and fired toward the portico, covering Zulu and George as they made their runs, subguns blazing.

George was faster than Zulu. Outdistancing the towering black man, he skidded down beside Track. "Jeez, how many of 'em are there?" he exclaimed.

"I don't know," Track answered, firing out the Uzi's magazine as Zulu finished his run and dropped into a low crouch beside Desiree.

"We must eliminate the fire from the portico if we are to penetrate the monastery while we still have men. I estimate we are outnumbered four to one," Zulu chimed in.

"Encouraging talk like that'll spoil me," Track grinned.

"I had planned that we might encounter heavy resistance," said Zulu as he reached to the backpack he wore. He shrugged out of the fabric straps and twisted around in his crouched position. He opened the pack.

"Hot damn," George exclaimed. The pack was filled with fragmentation grenades, and from the faded color he guessed they might be World War II vintage.

"Those things still work?" Track asked incredulously.

Zulu glanced at Track and smiled, "I shouldn't care to withdraw the pin, release the handle, and sit with one on my lap, major."

Track reached into the bag and snatched up one of the grenades. He pulled the safety pin and glanced toward the portico, then toward Zulu. "Watcha say the three of us guys try and impress the lady here—see who's the best pitcher, huh?"

George laughed, and grabbed up a grenade.

Emotionlessly, Zulu took one of the grenades.

Desiree took a fourth grenade. "I'm a liberated woman," she retorted. "I can throw a grenade as well as any of you."

Track started to smile, then broke into a grin.

"All right, everybody pull your pins, then when I say so, throw 'em." George, Zulu, then Desiree pulled the safety pins in the grenades.

"I never threw a grenade before," George admitted. "They don't show you how to do that kinda stuff in the Air Force."

"Rather like pitching at cricket," Zulu observed.

Track eyed the portico. There were at least ten of the enemy force up there, firing down. "Count of three," he murmured. "One...two...THREE!" Track's right arm hauled back then snapped forward, his hand letting loose the grenade. His eyes caught the dark blurs of motion as the other three grenades were tossed. He threw himself over Desiree, half to protect her and half because he liked to touch her.

The four grenades detonated almost simultaneously with a thundering roar. Track's ears were ringing as fragments of rock and centuries of dust rained down on them. He gripped Desiree tightly.

When the deadly ragged-edged chunks of stone had stopped flying, Track looked up. The hole beneath the mezzanine balcony that had been the portico was a mass of rock-strewn rubble, and all firing from the portico had ceased.

Track was up in an instant, springing onto the stone steps. Across the monastery confines he shouted in Greek, *"Pameh! Pameh!"*

He ran up the steps, firing his Uzi toward the mezzanine where there was a concentration of terrorist gunmen. Off to his right he heard the sound of more grenades exploding against the far section of the monastery confines. Somewhere behind him George shouted, "Uncle Dan, heads up, grenade." Track threw himself against the wall.

"Be more specific, George," Track shouted to his nephew as he wheeled around. George had grenades visibly stuffed in all his pockets.

"Gimme two, quick!" George grabbed one from his left front pocket, like a tennis player would retrieve a spare ball, and tossed it. Track caught it with his right, shifted it to his left, then caught the second grenade.

Track had a target. He looked at the grenade in his right fist. He raised the grenade toward his mouth and wrenched at the pin with his teeth. He'd always wanted to try it, ever since he had seen John Wayne do it in the movies. "Ouch—shit!" he yelled. He'd almost broken his right canine. But the pin was out, and he hauled back his hand, tossed and shouted, "Duck, George!"

Track felt the concussion, then shifted the second

grenade to his right fist. This time he pulled the pin with the fingers of his left hand. "So much for the movies," he grinned, as he threw the grenade toward a cluster of six men armed with assault rifles at the far end of the mezzanine.

An explosion flashed, and debris poured down. As the dust settled enough to see through, he realized all six men were out.

*"Pameh!"* he shouted to the Greek smugglers crouched on the stone steps behind him, firing their sub-guns. The men jumped and followed Track as he ran forward, the gunfire from the enemy positions throughout the stone monastery lighter now, more sporadic.

Desiree was beside him, firing an Uzi, while Track emptied his toward two of the terrorists crouched behind a broken stone pew.

A corridor ran off the far side of the mezzanine, and Track started toward it.

More assault rifle fire blazed from the far end of the corridor, and Track slammed against the wall at the corner feeding into the hallway. He dragged Desiree in beside him and shouted to Zulu, "You take Desiree back the way we came, pick up a couple of men along the way. Cut back through the courtyard. Take Adrianos with you if he's still alive out there—he came in with George. George and I will fight our way through the corridor here and we can link up, maybe catch some of them between us."

"Agreed, major," Zulu nodded. Then he reached into the pack that now slung by his massive left shoulder. He tossed two grenades to George and two to Track. "Dark of the moon as they say in commando circles." Looking at Desiree he added, "Come, Miss Desiree."

"I'll cover you," Track shouted, and he started to pump 3-round bursts from the Uzi around the corner and down the corridor.

"Tell me when they're clear," he shouted to George, "and get two other men if we got them."

"Right," George called back.

Track licked his lips. They were dry, but his palms were wet with sweat inside his gloves.

"They're clear," he heard George yell, "and I've got one man. All we've got left are two more and they're holding the far side of the mezzanine beside the steps."

Track glanced at his nephew and nodded. He looked at the Greek smuggler. He didn't remember his name. "Speak English?" he asked.

"Little part," the man smiled.

"Wonderful," Track nodded. "Stick with us and you'll talk English like a pro, fella."

Track rammed a fresh stick up the butt of the Uzi's pistol grip, fired a short burst, then darted around the corner and into the corridor. He zigzagged from one side to the other, drawing fire intentionally, counting on George behind him. Two men held a position at the far end of the corridor near a ramp, assault rifles blazing. Track went into a diving roll across the corridor. He came up on his knees, and fired a long ragged burst from his Uzi. Gunfire echoed from behind him as well, and both men at the far end of the corridor went down.

Track got to his feet and flattened himself against the wall, changing sticks for the Uzi. He had two left counting the one he had just inserted.

In a moment, George and the anonymous Greek were behind him along the wall.

Dotting both sides of the corridor were openings, perhaps at one time cells for the monks who had lived in the monastery. "You and our pal here, hit the far end of the corridor, there's a ramp there," instructed Track. "See where it leads. I'll check these rooms and keep an eye on your backs. Now, move out!"

George nodded, a cigarette burning out of the left

corner of his mouth. "I figured smoking couldn't be as hazardous to my health as what I'm doing now—may as well die happy and polluted." George looked at the Greek. "*Pameh*, buddy?"

George fired a test burst toward the end of the corridor, and ran off with the Greek close on his heels.

Track dropped the second Uzi, empty, to the corridor floor. He didn't need the extra weight.

He moved along slowly, and stopped at the first opening. A curtain covered it. He reached around from the side of the opening, tempted to lob a grenade through the curtained doorway. Instead, he ripped at the curtain, tearing it half away from where nails held it in place in the surrounding framework. There was no gunfire, no sound from inside.

He took one of his grenades and, leaving the pin in, rolled it through the doorway. There were no panicked shouts, no gunfire, no mad escapes through the doorway.

Cautiously, he stepped inside and watched the harmless grenade roll across the rough stone floor. He followed it with his eyes to the bed. He started forward. A naked woman lay face down on the bed, a hint of blueness in the veins in her neck. She wasn't moving.

Track rolled the body over onto its back, noticing that all the hair from the top of the head and the back of the neck was gone, apparently cut away.

The woman was very obviously dead—strangled, he surmised from the marks over the center of her throat.

"Hair," Track whispered. He looked about the room. Drawers in a battered chest were half open, and women's clothing and undergarments fell from them. A few pieces of clothing lay on the floor.

He left the bedside and walked toward the chest. There was a wooden-framed mirror on it, more than big enough for a woman to use to apply makeup. A few open jars littered the top of the chest. He picked one up. It was some type of blusher, a brand of cosmetics he didn't recognize. An eyebrow pencil with the cap off, and an open tube of mascara were scattered around. He pulled off his right glove and touched the mascara brush. It was wet.

He walked back across the room and felt at the woman's closed eyelids.

The eyelashes had no mascara.

The hair. The clothes. The makeup.

"My God!" Track shouted. "Krieger is Marlena now."

He ran from the room. Krieger was still on the island. He had to be, Track told himself.

As she jumped over the dead body of one of the terrorists, she felt the reassuring touch of Zulu's hand at her left elbow.

"Miss Desiree," he said, running beside her into the empty courtyard. "I will take you to safety. There are still...."

"We have to cut off the escape route from the far side of the courtyard," she interrupted. "Dan was right. It's the only way to get a line on the warheads."

"But Miss Desiree," came the stern reply. Suddenly she felt him grab at her left shoulder and pull her back, binding her behind him with his powerful left arm as he loosed a burst from his Uzi.

Two men went down. He turned to her quickly. "It is not..." he started.

"Safe—I know," she said, then started to run again, feeling slightly breathless. Fighting temporarily for the side of goodness and light amused her. She had not been in battle since the days in Africa, and Zulu, as he was now, had been beside her there, too.

She ran ahead to the far side of the courtyard. A

quick backward glance told her that two of the men from her smuggling vessel were still with her.

She slowed and let Zulu go first into the exit that led out of the courtyard. She covered him, knowing he could better handle what might be waiting there than she could.

When it came, it came so fast, she didn't realize it was happening at all. A burst of gunfire flashed from above the monastery and Zulu's body crumpled to the floor. He had been hit in the shoulder and side.

Ignoring the danger, she ran to Zulu's side, shielding him with her body.

She raised his head. "Miss Desiree...I...." Zulu faltered, and his eyes closed.

She swallowed hard, feeling at his neck for a pulse. He was alive, but quickly going into shock. Her gloved hands were covered with blood as she moved them from his back, his neck streaked with blood where she had touched him. She bent over him, and brushed her lips against his high forehead.

Desiree looked up to the parapets of the monastery. Silhouetted in the moonlight, she could see one man and a woman running. She watched their path down a track so rugged a mountain goat would have trouble traversing it. She guessed that it led to the sea, toward the rear of the monastery behind the pillars of rock.

Desiree looked up at Adrianos from where she knelt beside the bloodied and silent Zulu. "Take care of him with your life. Get to Major Track—get him to go," and she gestured to the other man. "George is big enough to carry Zulu. Track can fly a plane. We can get Zulu to Crete, to the hospital at Iráklion where I know the chief surgeon." She stood up, assessing the spare magazines for her borrowed Uzi—borrowed from a dead man.

She had three, plus the nearly full one in the submachine gun. "I'm going after them," she said, her face set and her eyes flashing with revenge.

"Miss Desiree," Adrianos stammered.

"I'm going after them. That woman is Marlena Fields, the one we came after. And the man may be Krieger. Now hurry, tend to Zulu and send for help—now!" she commanded.

Holding the Uzi in an assault position at her hip, she started to walk forward, breaking into a run after a few steps. She could cut across the rugged terrain and through the stone towers, then down to the sea. She would kill the man, whoever he was, the man with the woman Marlena. Because the man had held a rifle—and he had shot Zulu.

She owed Zulu nothing less. . . .

SHE WAITED IN THE SHADOWS of the rocks. Fire was visible in splotches of dark orange trailing skyward from the monastery, she didn't know the origins. She heard no gunfire, only the roar of the surf, the lapping of the waves and the throbbing of the seaplane's engine perhaps a hundred yards out. There was a launch waiting in the cove, waiting for the single man and the woman who accompanied him down through the rocks as she watched. For a moment, she thought of Zulu, and wondered whether Track and George had been found to carry Zulu to a doctor. Would Track leave the island without her? She hoped that he would.

"Dan," she whispered, barely moving her lips in the darkness. It was strange that she should love such a man. He was essentially a policeman. He had been one for the United States Army, tracking smugglers, gunrunners and murderers for the Criminal Investigation Division.

And now for this insurance cartel, the Consortium. Track was chasing potentially the greatest murderer in history, Johannes Krieger, the neo-Nazi, the right-wing terrorist, the master of disguise, whose real face no one knew.

"And his bitch," she murmured, watching Marlena as she stepped from the cover of the rocks. She was wearing a red high-fashion jogging suit, and a shawl partially obscured her face.

She was a tall woman, but moved gracefully.

Desiree Goth held her breath, and waited.

The man had straight blond hair, and there was a very Germanic look about him. Perhaps it was Krieger in another clever disguise. Maybe that was his real face—if it were Krieger.

Desiree stepped from the shadows, pumping the trigger of the Uzi, screaming at the man with the rifle as she killed him. "For Zulu, you bastard!"

The man's body crumpled to the rocks inches from Marlena's feet.

Before Marlena could move, Desiree had shifted the muzzle of the Uzi to cover her. "I'd love to kill you," Desiree screamed across the twenty yards separating them. "Stay perfectly still and you stay alive."

"Yes—I will," came the soft reply.

Desiree walked slowly, cautiously picking her way over the rocks, keeping the muzzle of the Uzi trained on Marlena's midsection.

Five yards from Marlena, she stopped. "Now, drop your purse to the rocks," she ordered.

Marlena obeyed.

"Now, very slowly, turn around. Remember—any sudden movement and you die, even the littlest thing, darling," cautioned Desiree. She almost wished Marlena would move, would give her an excuse to put her away with the Uzi. But she knew that Marlena might be their only link to Krieger.

Marlena slowly turned. Desiree approached to within

an arm's length of her, and started to feel at her waist for weapons. Suddenly, Marlena moved, faster than Desiree had thought any woman could move, the right hand sawing through the air, a knife cutting toward the muzzle of the Uzi.

Desiree stumbled back, letting herself fall to the rocks, guiding the muzzle clear of Marlena's quick reflexes. She fired a burst into the ground near Marlena's feet.

Marlena froze.

"Try that again and I'll kill you, darling, so help me I will." Desiree, slowly pushed herself to her feet. "Now, if you won't let me search you for weapons, we'll do it another way. Strip," she instructed.

There was a quiver of movement in what she could see of Marlena's face past the folds of the shawl.

Marlena whispered, "Very well, Fräulein Goth."

Desiree felt a smile cross her lips. "First the shawl, so I can see your face."

Marlena's left hand moved slowly, carefully, touching at the shawl with the tips of her fingers. As the shawl was whisked away, Desiree Goth screamed. The blond hair came away with it.

A man's face was suddenly staring at her, heavily made up with cosmetics.

She took a step closer and saw the set of the eyes.

It had to be Johannes Krieger. In a shaft of moonlight that lit the cove, she could see the ragged shape of a scar beneath his left earlobe.

She was suddenly mesmerized by the scar and the muzzle of the Uzi sagged in her hands for an instant.

There was a blur of motion, and Desiree felt a sharp pain and then nothing, except the sensation of falling into darkness.

ONE OF THE GREEKS had found a LAW rocket and had set out to the cove where Desiree had gone five minutes ahead of Track. Track, his shins aching and his lungs burning from oxygen depletion, stumbled over the broken ground, barely keeping his footing.

"Desiree," he gasped.

That Adrianos hadn't simply punched her in the jaw to stop her was unthinkable.

George was back with Zulu, giving basic first aid. The huge black man had multiple wounds across his shoulder and side, but Track's experience with gunshot wounds led him to think that none of them necessarily had to prove fatal.

Suddenly, he had heard shots from the cove, a single burst of automatic weapons fire, cracking like 9mms from a submachine gun.

He reached the top of the promontory overlooking the cove.

Beneath him, heading out to sea, was a motor launch. He couldn't see the occupants, but there was a male shape at the wheel. One of the seaplanes was airborne in the distance, and Track guessed the plane had taken off during the fighting. Now the occupants of the launch were making for the open sea.

On the cove, there was no sign of Desiree.

Track started down through the rocks, jumping from one flat piece to another to save a second here, a second there, running where he could.

The Greek was already in the cove.

Track could see the man shouldering the tube of the LAW rocket. "No!" He screamed the word, losing his balance, skidding, slipping and falling on the rocks. He raised his head and started to shout. But the shout was lost. The LAW rocket fired, and a whoosh of steamy white smoke erupted from the rear of the tube as it snaked seaward.

Track followed it with his eyes.

The motor launch seemed to hesitate for a moment.

Then it exploded into a storm cloud of billowing white smoke and then an orange and black fireball.

"Desiree! No!" Track shouted the words, and heard them echo off the rocks of the cove around him. The aircraft was too far out to have picked up anyone from the launch. Maybe she was already aboard the plane, he lied to himself.

He watched the burning wreckage of the launch settle on the otherwise-calm surface of the Aegean.

She was lost to him.

"Desiree," he whispered, for the first time truly understanding the full meaning of her name.

**15**

In what passed for an American bar in Iráklion on the island of Crete, Track sat drinking a Canadian-blended whiskey he'd never even heard of. With Adrianos, he had flown Zulu to the hospital to be operated on by the surgeon Desiree had referred to. The chief surgeon—Track had learned the man's name and forgotten it just as quickly—had veritably leapt at the mention of her name, recognizing Zulu instantly and personally making the arrangements for emergency surgery.

Track had waited there for three hours while bullet fragments were picked from the black man's muscles and flesh.

Zulu lived.

Track had left George on the island to search for Desiree. Hoping against hope that somehow she had not been aboard the launch.

But when the Greek who had fired the LAW rocket reached the cove, the plane had already been airborne, and the launch moving out of the cove had at least one person in it. Maybe two.

Footprints only small enough for Desiree's or another woman's had been found in a patch of sand.

Track took another swallow of whiskey.

Perhaps George would work a miracle and find her somehow. He should soon know.

He closed his eyes, not really believing that such a miracle would happen.

He heard a voice, but it wasn't a miracle, only his nephew.

He opened his eyes, and turned around. "The doctor must've told ya, right?" he asked.

George nodded. "Yeah, said you'd asked for the name of a bar that sold something besides ouzo."

"You didn't find any sign of her, right?" Track almost stated rather than asked.

George said nothing for a moment, then sat down beside Track at the bar. "A guy who was aboard Desiree's fishing boat," he said quietly, haltingly, "is a pretty good diver. At first light he went down and I guess the island shelves were out pretty far from the cove. The guy said it looked volcanic, the formation. He found part of the ship, the little launch. No bodies, but he found this," and George pulled something out of his pocket. His fist was closed on the bar, then he opened it.

In his palm was a yellow-gold ladies' Rolex wristwatch. It was still ticking, nearly eleven a.m. Encircling the face were tiny diamonds, each stone looking perfect in the dim light that emanated from behind the bar. The band was woven of twisted golden strands.

Tears welled up in Track's eyes, and he looked away from the watch to his nephew's face. "That's Desiree's watch," he said in a low, hoarse whisper. Track put his head against George's shoulder and let the tears come freely—he had no choice.

If Desiree had been on the boat, only one logical addendum presented itself. If Krieger had been on the island, and only he would have killed Marlena and substituted himself for the dead woman in order to preserve anonymity and effect an escape, then Krieger was dead also.

It was another bar, many miles away across the Aegean, and Track sat there with George beside him.

He could not return to the United States yet. Miles Jefferson had warrants out for his arrest there and Chesterton had been unable to squelch them. And if Krieger were dead, ninety-nine 500-kiloton nuclear warheads were out in the world waiting for someone to find them or some irresponsible person to use them. According to current estimates, it would take only a precious few of them, judiciously placed, to precipitate perhaps the end of all human life.

And the woman he loved, the only woman he had ever loved, was dead, not even enough of her body to be found to bury or cremate.

He drank very little. He had no heart for it. It would make him feel his sadness all the more.

He was very tired.

His weapons had come in from the United States, as had George's. What good were they? he wondered. The SPAS-12, perhaps the finest police shotgun yet devised. The M-16 with "Potentiameter" adjustable aimpoint sight. The Metalife Custom L-Frame stainless Smith & Wesson .357 Magnum revolver. The Trapper Scorpion .45. Chesterton, on Track's casual request, had secured two Walther P-5 9mm as well. Track was taken with the gun based on its performance in Austria and on the island near Crete.

But what good were any of these? Madmen now ran the asylum called Earth and soon would destroy it, bringing the asylum down around them.

And the woman he loved—had loved would never be the phrase—was dead, gone from his touch.

He set down his drink, looked at George, then quietly said, "I'm going up to the room. Maybe I can sleep or something."

George returned the look. "Don't punch me out, but maybe you should find a girl and. . . ."

"No," Track told him. "No, it wouldn't do any good."

"Hey, Uncle Dan. Look, I'm sorry, really I am."

Track slapped his nephew's shoulder. "If I ever tell you you're like a son to me again, hit me, okay? But you are. Thanks." And Track stood up and walked away from the bar, sticking George with the check. . . .

He turned the key with difficulty in his door. Maybe he had drunk a little too much, he thought. As he walked in, he smelled the cigarette smoke and instinctively started back through the door, but the voice, a voice he recognized, whispered, "major, it is your old friend Sergei. You recall, your shot broke my ski."

He was caught cold and he knew it. So he laughed and said, "I was trying to shoot you in the ass and I missed, Baslovitch."

TRACK SMOKED ONE OF the Cuesta Rey Six-T's, Baslovitch a cigarette, a British Players.

Baslovitch's Heckler & Koch P-7, one of the finest 9mms to be had and perhaps the safest to operate, lay on the table next to the pack.

"So, what do you want?" Track asked him.

"My sympathies," Baslovitch began. "I did some homework on you, major. My sympathies for the death of the woman Desiree. She was beautiful, but I'm sure you valued her for more than that."

"Thank you," Track answered sincerely. "I did value her for more than that." He added, "I do—still."

"Why didn't you kill me, major?" asked Baslovitch.

Track shrugged his shoulders. "I was trying to put you out of the action, that's all. If you go out of your way to kill people, you're either an idiot or a psychotic, unless you're a professional assassin, of course, and that's your business interest. Anyway, you kinda hate putting away someone you just fought beside."

"Perhaps our two nations need a common enemy and

could adopt such a philosophy themselves," Baslovitch suggested.

"Perhaps," Track agreed. "Who knows, maybe we'll be invaded by three-eyed green guys from Alpha Centuri or something."

"A cheerful prospect," Baslovitch said with a laugh.

Track started to crack a smile as he shrugged. "So, if you didn't come to kill me, and you could have tried when I came in the room...."

"I could have succeeded, major," Baslovitch smiled.

"Could have tried," Track insisted good-naturedly. "But then why did you come?"

"Shall we accept the fact that neo-Nazis hate communism as much as they hate democracy?" Baslovitch began.

"Sure, we can accept that fact," agreed Track.

"Well, then you know why I came, at least partially. When I mentioned the death of the woman, I was taking unfair advantage of you, but I had to," Baslovitch said.

"I don't understand," Track said flatly.

"Testing your mettle, as the English say. I wanted to know what sort of man I would be dealing with. But I feel sorry about having done it that way," the Russian continued.

"What?" Track interrupted, not following Baslovitch's train of thought.

"All right," and Baslovitch leaned across the table. "I was able to follow your progress to the little island where Marlena Fields had her hideaway. I watched what transpired from the water, had myself launched from the torpedo tube of one of our smaller classes of nuclear submarine well off shore. So I watched, but I was powerless to stop it. I want that clear."

"You mean you watched while Desiree was killed?" Track whispered hoarsely.

"No. Your Desiree Goth confronted a man and a woman on the beach, killed the man and was disarming the woman," confided Baslovitch. "But the woman was not a woman, and the...."

"Wait a minute," Track interrupted.

"Desiree Goth was knocked to the ground by someone who could only have been Johannes Krieger," stated Baslovitch. "Then Krieger hauled the body of the dead man into the power launch. He set the launch on a course out of the cove and dived into the water. I started inland. I'd been watching from a quarter mile offshore with vision-intensification binoculars—the sort of thing we used to do when we spied on your country's space program launches from Cape Kennedy. Swim in, use a flotation device so you can keep your head above water and utilize a camera or some other technique of direct visual observation. He got Desiree to her feet and they moved out beyond the cove toward the other side of the island. Then that man appeared with the LAW rocket and destroyed the boat. The plane was airborne as soon as the launch left the cove. I assume the pilot figured to hell with waiting for Krieger or Marlena, he'd save his own skin. But Desiree was alive when I saw her taken off by Krieger. And she saw his face, I know that. She may still be alive."

Track leaned back in his chair, clasping his hands over his eyes. He listened as Baslovitch, the Russian's voice a hush, continued talking.

"I'm a good swimmer. I almost competed for my country in the Olympics, but to cover the quarter mile or so to the shore, then make a dead run and catch Krieger was impossible. A lot of planes got airborne from the far side of the cove, and I assumed Krieger was on one of the seaplanes and probably took your Desiree Goth with him. You wanted to know why I was interested in all of this. For a very special reason. There is a neo-Nazi underground at work within the Soviet Union. Some of these people are highly placed, we suspect. If Krieger has your warheads, the ninety-nine that remain—'' Track looked up at the Russian, studying the man's eyes, the Russians knew ''—well, we have reason to believe that if his first attempt at a detonation was in the United States, his second may be in the Soviet Union. He is our common enemy, and I am authorized to propose that we work together to stop him, whatever it takes.''

"Hmm," Track murmured.

"You no doubt wonder why the Soviet Union has not taken advantage of the knowledge of the missing warheads, perhaps attacked your country because one hundred 500-kiloton warheads are off line," Baslovitch ventured.

"The thought has crossed a few minds, I think," conceded Track.

"A simple reason, really," stated the Russian. "Despite occasional rumors to the contrary, we're not any more insane than yourselves, nor any more interested in possibly ending all life on earth. Fifty-thousand kilotons sounds like a great deficiency in U.S. nuclear strength, yet fifty megatons is not. And of course the figures are one in the same.''

"What do you want me to say?" Track asked him. Thoughts of Desiree, being still alive, and perhaps the captive of Johannes Krieger, filled his mind to the point where he couldn't think, couldn't rationally consider Baslovitch's words.

"A partnership, however uneasy? Until this matter is resolved?" suggested Baslovitch.

Track noticed that his cigar had gone out. He studied it a moment, forcing himself to think. After what he realized was a very long silence, he looked up from the extinguished tip of the cigar.

"I can't speak for Chesterton and the Consortium," he replied. "I can't even speak for my nephew George. And certainly not for the United States government."

He paused again, unconsciously, then continued, "But for myself—to stop Krieger, to maybe find Desiree Goth—for myself, yes."

THE U.S. WARRANTS were killed. Miles Jefferson had announced that as he entered the room, also announcing that after it was all over he planned to punch out Dan Track. George's uncle had countered by saying Jefferson had no sense of humor.

George sat to his uncle's right, at the long dining-room table in a house just outside Athens. The house was owned by one of the member companies of the Consortium and used by the company's corporate staff for vacations. George felt it was too elaborate to be comfortable. With at least twenty rooms and decorated like something out of a movie about the right and powerful, the place gave him the creeps.

He looked at the others around the table. Directly opposite him sat Sergei Baslovitch, the Russian whose offer had sparked the meeting. Beside him, drawn away as though communism were a contagious disease, was Miles Jefferson. At the head of the table sat Sir Abner Chesterton.

The rest of the table, with space for perhaps two dozen people, was empty. A cut flower arrangement stood at the center, and an elaborate, lace-trimmed runner had been rolled back from the section of the table they now occupied.

Sir Abner Chesterton spoke. "I think, Agent Jefferson, your remarks suggesting physical retribution were a bit uncalled for. I would hazard the guess that under similar circumstances you and Dan Track would have behaved in a similar fashion. And for the moment, at least, your country and Major Baslovitch's country have informally agreed to work together to stop a common threat. An historic moment, certainly, and an historic beginning, perhaps. What we have, gentlemen,'' and now Chesterton made a sweeping gesture with his hands, encompassing all those who sat at the massive table, ''is the opportunity of foiling Johannes Krieger by sheer force of numbers.

"I was in contact earlier today with Mr. Zulu, Miss Goth's associate. From his hospital bed in Iráklion on the island of Crete, he is managing Miss Goth's considerable financial concerns and business matters. He has, as I'd had no reason to suspect the contrary, pledged Miss Goth's considerable sources and contacts to watch for Krieger and of course any evidence of Miss Goth." George watched as Chesterton looked for an instant to Dan.

"Suffice it to say," Chesterton continued, "with the criminal community watching, with the Soviet Union watching over its own considerable spheres of influence and the United States and selected allies—Her Majesty's Government a particular case in point—joining in, we have the world's ports, air terminals and other transportation systems under scrutiny. To perpetrate his foul deeds, Johannes Krieger must likely travel, since he seems to prefer a personal touch. Ergo, he'll surface and one of our people, from whatever source, may spot him."

"You forget, Sir Abner," Baslovitch began. "The matter of Krieger's face. We do not know it. He could be anyone."

"I daresay, you're quite correct, Major Baslovitch. He could even be one of us." Chesterton smiled.

George watched his uncle. Dan Track didn't smile at all.

## 16

She realized that she was still alive only because the man the world sought as Johannes Krieger hadn't known she had seen the scar. Otherwise, he could not have let her live.

Naked except for the torn and dirty pink silk teddy she had worn under her clothes during the assault on the island, she sat with her legs tucked up on a packing crate, watching the rats move about the floor. It wasn't terribly bad, she reflected. During the daylight hours, a few shafts of light made it possible at least to see in the cargo hold where she was kept. But at night it was a different story. That was when the rats represented terror to her. While she had dozed, one of them came at her. She had felt it against the sole of her bare left foot and she screamed. Perhaps because of the scream or her sudden motion, the rat had been frightened away.

She had not slept since, and she judged it as thirty-six hours at least. Her watch had been taken from her at some point between the time Krieger had knocked her out and then forced her along to the other side of the island after reviving her.

Krieger had apparently had his own escape route planned all the while. When she had seen the launch explode, he told her the man with the LAW rocket hadn't given his explosive charge time to work. He had planted it on the launch the previous day in the event Marlena Fields betrayed him. A small boat had been hidden in an inlet and they had taken the boat out to sea, where one of the seaplanes picked them up. After a short flight, they landed near the dark hulk of what she guessed was either an Albanian or East German freighter. After that, Krieger had stripped off her clothes and locked her away.

There were no toilet facilities except for a galvanized mop bucket and this was changed every eight hours or so. It was her only way of keeping time. It was impossible to keep track by the tiny cracks of light that squeezed through slits in the overhead cargo doors. She knew that the ship was in motion. The rocking had made her nauseated.

She glanced up at the cracks in the doors. The light was nearly gone. Her head buzzed, her eyes stung with fatigue. Another night quickly approached. If she slept, she thought, the rats would come and chew at her flesh.

The side door of the cargo hold opened, and the rats scurried for cover amid the packing crates.

A man, tall and clean shaven except for a thin mustache, quickly entered the hold. He was handsome by any standards. "I have come to rescue you," the man began, sprinting across the room. "I work for Sir Abner Chesterton—no time to explain," the very British voice urged. "Hurry, I'll get you out of here." The man handed her a raincoat. She climbed down from the crates and stood up, covering herself with it. "It's all I have for you, I'm afraid, but from the looks of this hole a good hot tub might be in order as soon as I've got you out of here."

"Who are you?" she whispered, wrapping the trench coat around her waist, staring at the man's gray eyes. "Where did you come from?" With sandy-colored hair, and the patrician nose he looked like the hero of a romance novel.

"My name is David Stearns, and let's just say the old-boy network still functions when it can, shall we?"

From under his coat, he pulled out a pistol. She recognized it as a Walther PPK. "I'm afraid one pistol was all I could bring, Miss Goth. Now, hurry, we've not much time before that guard I coshed might come around and raise an alarm."

"Yes," she whispered, her spirits rising. The British Secret Service—the old-boy network was a common euphemism for it. The man, athletic, tall and wiry, raced across the cargo bay with Desiree at his heels.

He flattened himself against the door for a moment, then glanced at her and smiled. "Stiff upper lip, Miss Goth. We're nearly there. Come on!" He opened the door just wide enough to squeeze out. She followed him, the metal floor slippery and cold under her bare feet. She noticed his clothes—a black and gray herringbone tweed jacket, expensively cut, a black silk-knit tie, oxford gray slacks and loafers. A white shirt. He looked perfect for what he was, she thought.

David Stearns was at the base of a metal stairway. Desiree huddled behind him. "Your Major Track has been terribly worried over you," the man said with a warm smile. "But you should be in his arms soon."

"And Zulu?" She asked, hesitating, "did he. . . ?"

"The black chap? In a hospital at Iráklion and mending nicely, Miss Goth," came the reply. "Now, mum while we take the stairs lest they raise an alarm. Hurry." Stearns started up the steps, two at a time. Desiree, holding the handrail, followed.

Fresh air. As she inhaled the salty-smelling breeze, she began to feel faint, but Stearns was at her elbow. "Steady on, Miss Goth. We're nearly free of this place."

"What about Krieger?" she asked.

"His whereabouts are known, but no one is moving against him until your safety is assured. Major Track himself would have been here, but I was the closest and circumstances wouldn't allow a delay."

She nodded, and moved after him, cautiously, slowly, seeing daylight through the opening to the main deck ahead.

In a hushed tone, her rescuer murmured, "Those chaps...I mean during your confinement...I hope you weren't, ahh. Deuced awkwardly, actually."

"No, thank God. They left me alone," said Desiree. She shivered as she said it.

And then David Stearns stopped, just below deck level, and turned to her. His eyes furled under the sandy-colored brows, he asked, "Did you see his face? Could you identify him?"

She thought of the scar, but evaded his question. "When I saw him, he was disguised as a woman named Marlena Fields. I think I saw his real hair color when he pulled away the shawl that covered his head. He was wearing something like a wig, and it didn't look like a real wig. More like he'd glued hair into the shawl. But the hair I saw underneath it could have been dyed. The face itself was too heavily made up to recognize."

"Hmm," he murmured, his lips turning down at the corners of his mouth. "Clever, this Krieger. Damn clever. Come on, and watch your footing." He was through the opening to the deck, Desiree moving along slightly behind him.

A helicopter waited on the main deck, its rotor blades moving lazily. "Is that for us?" Desiree Goth whispered.

David Stearns turned and pointed the Walther PPK at her abdomen. "I am afraid not, Fräulein Goth. It is for me alone."

Fear gripped her.

The voice was no longer the refined, British voice of David Stearns, but the voice of the man half in drag from the cove, the voice of her jailer. The voice of Johannes Krieger.

She threw herself toward him, hammering her fists against his chest when her nails couldn't gouge at his eyes.

But there were hands on her, roughly pulling her back. Seamen from the freighter bound her arms behind her.

She looked at Johannes Krieger. The face was still that of David Stearns. Makeup camouflaged the lightning-bolt-shaped scar beneath the left earlobe. She despised him, hated him.

She snapped her head forward, spitting at him. But she missed and Krieger laughed. She realized she had been beaten again.

She stared down toward the hold. Soon, it would be night. She couldn't stay awake any more. Her body and her mind had been punished enough. She screamed.

"We're not putting you back into the hold, Fräulein," soothed Krieger. "You're going on a journey. You may prove a useful bargaining tool against the Consortium, and Major Track in particular. I had to be certain you hadn't seen too much of me. I couldn't risk your being able to recognize me. And now I am certain."

"Where are you taking me?" she blurted out.

"I am taking you nowhere, Fräulein. But some of my associates are. I am going behind what the Western democracies call the Iron Curtain. A job there needs my personal touch. Just think of it," he said as he leaned toward her, smiling, his face inches from hers. She wanted to spit at him, but her mouth was too dry to attempt it again. "An American nuclear device detonated inside a vital area of the Soviet Union. They will be at each other's throats. And the stage will be set for the final move, one that shall bring both East and West to my feet."

He took a step back and laughed. Then in the voice of

David Stearns he said, "I must dash off, I'm afraid. But we'll see each other soon, Miss Goth. As our friends across the channel say, *au revoir*."

He turned and walked away. "Bastard!" Desiree Goth screamed at him. Then she felt the tip of the needle against her left upper arm as the raincoat was ripped away by one of the crewmen.

She passed out in somebody's arms.

JOHANNES KRIEGER STEPPED DOWN out of the helicopter, the wind created by the rotor blades whipping through his hair. It was his own hair, dyed and not a wig. He jogged from the still stirring machine across the concrete airfield. To his right, the desert sun was a blood-red orb sinking on the western horizon.

A Lear business jet sat waiting, the engines already humming with life as he narrowed the distance toward it. Slung from his left shoulder was a leather stuff sack. In his right hand was a matching leather flight bag.

He reached the steps of the jet, not even winded from the two-hundred yard sprint.

He started up the steps with a feeling of triumph. The fools had bought the idea that he would trust his operation to the dregs of the right wing, which Marlena Fields had assembled for him. The security there had been so lax, had they really thought he would be such a dolt?

He stowed his luggage in the small closet just aft of the cockpit, then stepped through the cockpit doorway and addressed the pilot.

"I shall be ready in a moment, please begin take-off," he commanded.

"Yes, Mr. Krieger," the American pilot answered him.

The copilot, looking very European, said nothing.

Krieger returned to the passenger compartment and picked out a seat. A very pretty young woman came forward. "Would you care for a drink, Mr. Krieger?" she asked. A slight German accent strayed through her otherwise faultless English.

Still in his British accent to go with the role of David Stearns, Krieger replied, "Yes, a gin and tonic would be most refreshing."

He swiveled his chair and watched her as she walked down the aisle. The plane was already taxiing. He glanced at the Omega on his left wrist. There would be time perhaps, he reflected, and the couch looked large enough for two.

He smiled, swiveled his seat, then locked it in position. The woman would be more refreshing than the gin and tonic. And there would be little time for refreshment in Russia.

## 17

George had not been legally able to come along. After his stint in Air Force Intelligence and with his security clearance still standing, permission was required to enter any Communist nation, and permission had been denied.

Track considered it just as well. It was good to know that George was on the outside in case the rosy relationship with Baslovitch and the KGB suddenly failed. He never doubted for an instant that George would find a way of getting him back out, or die trying.

He stood beside the car now, his personal weapons concealed on his body. The Metalife Custom L-Frame was in the Cobra rig under his left armpit, the little Trapper Scorpion .45 in the Alessi holster near his right kidney. The SPAS-12 and the rest of his gear were in Baslovitch's official car.

He watched as Baslovitch conversed with the apparent leader of a Soviet navy scuba team. He imagined they were something like the U.S. Navy SEALS, commandos whether functioning on land or water. Each man carried a fighting knife strapped to his left leg, and a waterproof pack slung over his back, some obviously containing assault rifles. He imagined others carried explosives and other gear. Each diver also carried a holster on his weight belt, the holster apparently constructed of plastic and able to seal water tight. He figured these were for a stainless steel variant of the Makarov, but he had yet to see one. The bright-blue flippers all the men wore seemed incongruous against their jet black wet-suits.

Track shrugged. Maybe it was just faulty color coordination.

There seemed to be a final word between Baslovitch and the commander, then the two men formally shook hands and Baslovitch started to move up from the small inlet back toward the car. The frogmen started into the water, moving in a wedge formation.

A little out of breath, Baslovitch laughed, "They are ready, they move out for the assault." As he gestured behind him, the diver's heads and shiny, silver-colored scuba tanks disappeared beneath the incoming tide.

It had been mere hours since the meeting in the home outside Athens where word had come in that a Soviet submarine near the Strait of Otronto had spotted a helicopter taking off from an East German ship. The ship had been not far from Albania's coastal city of Sarande.

It had been impossible to monitor the movements of the helicopters, but keeping the freighter under surveillance the submarine's commander had reported seeing a large object hauled aboard a seaplane, which had landed near the freighter. Again, tracking the aircraft was impossible as it often proved, Track thought, with small planes. It was why such aircraft were favorites among smugglers the world over.

But tracking the ship as it progressed the modest distance toward Sarande had not been difficult.

Track got into the Moscva beside Baslovitch. The Russian put a lead foot on the gas peddle as he sped away. "We rendezvous with our helicopter in ten minutes," he said, not lifting his eyes from the road, "and it's a fifteen-minute drive at normal speeds. Then we're airborne and move in toward the ship."

"What's the name of the ship?" Track wanted to know.

"Do you speak German?" Baslovitch inquired.

"I get by," Track said absently. He'd at least learned something during his years in CID in Germany.

"It is *Das Wunderkind*," Baslovitch said.

"The Wonderchild?" said Track.

"Perhaps prodigy might be a better term in English," Baslovitch suggested. "We will attack the Wonderchild at precisely on the hour. Twenty-three minutes from now, allowing three minutes for the underwater personnel to take their positions for an assault on the ship. As our helicopter closes in and hopefully distracts them, the men will swarm up the sides. The first order of business is, of course, any warheads and keeping Fräulein Goth alive."

"In that order," Track murmured soberly.

"In that order," Baslovitch echoed.

Track stared out the passenger window, trying to remain calm, but not succeeding.

Baslovitch began to talk, and Track guessed it was as a kindness to distract him. "Tell me, Dan, if I may call you that...."

"What? Sergei," Track nodded.

"Why is it that you left the service of your Army? Disenchantment?"

"Hardly," Track said, laughing. "Maybe disenchantment with Army life, maybe that. But not about what I was doing or why. Why do you ask? Having a few reservations about your own future?"

Baslovitch said nothing for a moment, then turned toward him for an instant, grinning broadly. "Suffice it to say, please think of me as your friend—and think of yourself as mine." He looked back to the road. Track was happy the Russian had done that—it was a winding, narrow road and Baslovitch was driving too fast. "In case I should ever have the need," Baslovitch added.

Track said nothing.

As THE TWIN ROTOR BLADES whirled overhead, Track set the SPAS-12 shotgun from pump to semi-auto mode. Beside him on the jump seats behind the pilot and the Soviet Naval liaison officer, Sergei Baslovitch, the KGB officer, checked the seating of a 30-round magazine in an AKM. Track unzipped the front of his brown leather bomber jacket so he could more easily get to the Metalife Custom L-Frame in the shoulder rig under his left armpit, or the Trapper Scorpion .45 behind his right kidney.

His palms sweated slightly inside his leather gloves, and the sensation made him remember to check the gloves themselves. Three Shuriken spikes were sheated on the back of each. He had the spikes custom-made, since finding them commercially was extremely difficult.

The outside patch pockets of the bomber jacket bulged with Federal hollow point slug loads and 12-gauge 2 3/4-inch double "O" Buck. Some of these were loaded alternately in the round tubular magazine of the SPAS, Buck up first. The pockets of his faded Levis bulged as well with Safariland speed-loaders for the L-Frame .357 revolver. On his belt, a double Alessi friction retention pouch carried two spare Detonics 8-round magazines for the Trapper Scorpion. Each of these was custom fitted to provide as close as possible a flawless feed with the Trapper .45.

He was ready, for all of it, he thought. But ready was such a nebulous term. One resigned oneself to facing death out of necessity, it was never something to take with complete calm.

He caught Baslovitch eyeing him. The Russian said, "I am always nervous before something like this. Death holds little appeal, especially as an atheist."

Track couldn't help but smile. He spoke into his headset microphone, looking at Baslovitch. "I'm not an atheist, but death isn't something I'm especially eager for either.'' Track took a cigar from inside his jacket, looked at it a moment, then put it away. Smoking was bad for the health. Hell, most of his friends said his Cuesta Reys were bad for the atmosphere for that matter.

Track rolled back the sleeve of his bomber jacket to look at the Rolex. He looked away from the face, and focused on Baslovitch's. The Russian nodded, and Track followed his look through the open fuselage doorway.

The superstructure amidships of the Wunderkind loomed on the horizon.

He heard Baslovitch's whisper through the headset microphone, ''The attack begins.''

Track only nodded. The SPAS-12's chamber was empty, and as soon as he hit the deck of the freighter, he would chamber the first round and the mini-war would start. He hoped the Soviet counterparts of SEALS made it up the sides of the hull quickly. The sweating inside his gloves had all but stopped.

The superstructure of the Wunderkind seemed higher now, more massive. The outlines of cargo-hold hatches were visible fore and aft, the radar mast and radar antennas towered above the bridge. Coming up from port he could make out the massive anchor, and just aft of the prow the windlass and mooring winch.

Track could see men moving on the deck as the Wunderkind came into still greater definition. The helicopter was obviously becoming more apparent to them now, and some of the deck personnel began to run. Track heard Baslovitch's voice, both through his headset and with an echo effect delay from the exterior speaker of the helicopter's PA System. He spoke in Russian, a language with which Track had only the most nodding familiarity. But Track knew the meaning—heave to, official business of the Soviet government and the Albanian government. There was the possibility the ship's personnel would offer no resistance to Soviet authority.

As Track heard the ricochet of a rifle bullet off the fuselage he dismissed that possibility entirely. "Oh, well," he sighed. He decided not to do it the safe way, and he chambered the first round out of the SPAS's magazine, set the trigger guard safety, and loaded an extra double "O" Buck from his jacket pocket into the magazine.

Track tucked back to gain whatever protection he could from the fuselage of the helicopter. Gunfire was streaming up toward them now from the deck, and Track watched as Baslovitch spoke to the pilot in English. Track assumed this was for his benefit, and over the phones he heard Baslovitch say "Between the amidships cargo holds, land us there, Captain!"

There was no answer from the pilot, and Track heard Baslovitch speaking again, this time in Russian.

He felt the helicopter bank hard to port, coming in at an angle toward the freighter. Track leaned forward past the meager protection of the fuselage, the Metalife Custom L-Frame in his right fist. A man with a machine gun stood amidships, just where the helicopter was heading. At the distance, a hundred yards and closing fast, the chopper was an easy target, but the man on the deck was a poor target for Track with the SPAS and double "O" Buck, a movie-shot target that no one in real life could make. But with a pistol it was marginally possible.

The memory-grooved Goncalo Alves stocks filled his right fist, and his right fist filled his left palm as his right thumb brought back the hammer.

The machine gunner was swinging on target. Track squeezed.

Nothing happened beyond the gun discharging.

"Shit," Track growled. The range was fifty yards now, and the machine-gun bullets beat a deadly tattoo against the fuselage. Baslovitch was shouting at the pilot in Russian, the helicopter started to veer off, then settled back on course.

Track could feel Baslovitch beside him. "My AKM—" Baslovitch shouted, his thundering voice overriding the headphones.

Track rasped, "Go ahead, if you still need to after this!"

Track settled the orange insert in the white-outlined rear notch of the L-Frame, the hammer back again. This time he made his body move with the movement of the chopper, and didn't fight it. He touched at the trigger just as the machine gun loosed a long burst of metallic death toward the chopper. The Plexiglas windshield spiderwebbed as the .357 rocked in Track's fists.

The machine gunner fell back from his weapon, hands and arms flailing, his body arced on the deck, twitching convulsively, then lay still.

Track heard Baslovitch shouting, "You did it, dammit, you did it!"

And then Track could feel the hot brass shell casings pelting at his face and neck as Baslovitch's AKM roared. The sound was deafening in the confined space of the helicopter's cabin, despite the earphones.

They were twenty yards from their selected landing area now, and closing fast. A man rushed up to the position of the dead machine gunner, firing a pistol. As he dropped to his knees at the gun emplacement, Track fired the L-Frame, double actioning it now at the distance. He caught the man somewhere in the chest, and the lifeless body snapped back from the machine gun, his white T-shirt sprayed with blood.

Track allowed himself a smile, but not at death. Death was nothing to enjoy. But he smiled because he could feel it—he was on a roll, shooting well. The fighting would be hard, perhaps deadly to him, but it would be a good fight. His muscles were pumping adrenaline and his senses were honed and sharp. He was into it.

He discharged the L-Frame twice more, and wounded a man running toward the machine gun emplacement.

He dumped his empties on the floor of the chopper, and rammed one of the Safariland cylinder-shaped speed-loaders against the L-Frame's ejector star, dumping six new rounds into the charging holes.

Pocketing the empty speed-loader—no sensible man threw them away, Track thought fleetingly—he reholstered the L-Frame.

His trigger finger edged against the safety of the SPAS, just inside the guard. The second safety was something he didn't bother with under combat conditions. And this was combat.

Track loosened his safety restraints as the helicopter started to settle.

With the helicopter still six feet off the deck, he yelled, "Go for it," into the headset and ripped it away.

Track launched himself from the side of the chopper, and went into a roll as he hit the deck, his trigger finger punching the SPAS's safety forward, then the finger snapping back.

He exploded a load of double "O" Buck into three men storming toward him with pistols. All three went down as the shot tore into their bodies, ripping away flesh and grinding up bone. Track fired again and a Federal hollow point exploded in another man's throat, setting off a geyser of blood. Behind him he heard the roar of Baslovitch's AKM.

Track hit the deck and rolled at the sound of subgun fire to his left. As he came to his knees he ripped off another round from the SPAS, and a grapefruit-sized hole appeared where the subgunner's chin had been a second before.

A machine gun opened up from the superstructure amidships.

Track launched himself forward, the deckplates under his feet echoing with the machine-gun slugs, the pattern catching up to him as he dived to the protection of some cargo crates lashed down and covered with a tarpaulin at the base of the superstructure.

The tops of the crates seemed to explode upward, and Track felt bits of fabric and slivers of wood pelting him.

He raised the SPAS, getting the muzzle leveled toward the superstructure and the machine-gun nest. He fired, then tucked back as a fresh burst of machine-gun fire hammered into the crates.

He could see Baslovitch pinned down less than twenty feet from the reach of the chopper's rotor blades. The chopper was starting to move, twisting, gaining perhaps a few inches of elevation.

He focused on the pilot—his body was slumped over the controls.

Track fired off a load of buckshot at maybe thirty yards. The machine gun fell silent, but then started again. Track's fingers dug in the right side pocket of the bomber jacket—Buck in the right pocket, slug in the left.

He started feeding them—one, two, three, four, five, six, seven, until he had a full magazine of shot and one hollowpoint in the chamber.

Track fired out the slug load toward the machine-gun nest, then was up and running, pulling the trigger of the SPAS as fast as he could as he raced toward the metal steps leading up to the superstructure. The SPAS was tensioned on its sling over his shoulder, the folded-out stock pressed rigidly against his right hip. Five loads of double "O" Buck spraying out in a rain of death, pinning down the machine gunner.

He reached the top of the steps and raced across the superstructure as the machine gunner started to turn his weapon around. Track dropped to his knees, sliding on the slick surfaced deck, firing the last round from the SPAS.

The machine gunner's face and most of the head seemed to disappear in a sunburst of blood, a chunk of something gray and blood-smeared separating from the top of the machine gunner's head and slapping back against the bulkhead.

Track let the empty SPAS fall to his side on its sling, and ran for the machine gun.

He caught a blur of motion to his right, and glanced over to see the wheelhouse door opening. Track's right hand snatched one of the Shuriken spikes from the back of his left glove. His hand snapped the stainless steel spike toward the target like a cobra making a strike. The man's body slammed back against the wheelhouse door as the deadly spike plunged into his chest, backflipping through the glass forming the upper panel.

Still part of the same motion, Track's right hand swept back to the butt of the Trapper Scorpion .45. As he brought it around, his right thumb swept down the ambidextrous safety, and his finger pumped the trigger, as he aimed the muzzle of the little pistol through the broken glass of the wheelhouse doorway.

He blew the magazine, and skidded like a base runner into position behind the machine gun.

It was a U.S. M-60. He kept finding stolen U.S. weapons everywhere, he thought. They obviously needed him back in CID, he laughed, and he swung the machine gun down toward the deck below.

He rammed one of the 8-round Detonics magazines into the Trapper, letting the slide slam forward. He set the pistol on the deck near his left hand, safety up. He was ready for an assault from behind.

He started firing the M-60 into the freighter's defenders. The Soviet scuba commandos began to swarm up over the sides of the hull now from port and starboard, pistols and assault rifles blazing.

Acting on a sixth sense more than anything else, Track whipped his left hand down to the deck for the Trapper .45. His left thumb flicked down the safety and he rammed the muzzle toward the wheelhouse. Two men ran out, one with an AKM. Track fired off four rounds and the AKM hit the deck in the hands of a dead man. The second man had a 9mm pistol, and Track felt the impact of a bullet against the mounts for the M-60, hearing the whine of a ricochet.

He fired the .45. It was called a Scorpion, and it stung the man with the pistol once in the chest and put him down.

He upped the safety, knowing that three rounds remained, and turned to the M-60 again, taking greater care now that the Soviet commandos were on board.

The long barrel of the M-60 was smoking from the strain. But Track kept pumping the trigger, firing 3- or 4-round bursts at specific targets of opportunity rather than spraying out saturation fire.

The Soviet commandos fought the crew of the freighter in hand-to-hand combat now. There was little automatic weapon fire. Track slumped back from the machine gun, then hauled up his left leg, his left foot against the gun. He shoved, letting the machine gun tumble from the superstructure to the main deck below, disabling it.

With the Trapper in his left fist and the Metalife L-Frame in his right, he started across the superstructure. Crewmen came at him from various openings, some turned and ran as they saw him, some wanted to fight. Track obliged.

He reached a companionway leading down into the

bowels of the ship, and stopped long enough to ram a fresh magazine in the Trapper, the last of the two spares.

The L-Frame still had four rounds in the cylinder, and he left it alone.

A tremendous explosion rocked Track back against the bulkhead. The helicopter that had been weaving skyward pilotless from the deck amidships tumbled over the portside railing in a spectacular fireball.

He could see Baslovitch coming toward the superstructure, the AKM in one hand, a little 9mm H&K pistol in his left.

Track started down into the companionway. If Desiree were somehow still aboard he would find her. No one would stop him.

He smelled gasoline ahead in the darkness as he reached the base of the metal treads.

He kept going, his eyes shut tight, counting to ten, opening them again, more accustomed to the light.

The gasoline smell was stronger now, almost nauseous. He turned an elbow bend in the darkened passageway. Ahead of him he could barely discern the outline of a male shape. "Freeze!" he shouted in English—it didn't matter. It was the sound, not the word in a situation like this.

The figure wheeled, and Track tucked against the bulkhead to his left, dodging as a tongue of flame licked out toward him from the darkness, a huge one, like the tongue of a monster.

The bulkhead beside him was suddenly scorched a deathly black as the passageway burst with the orange light of fire. It was a flame thrower. Track's blood ran cold.

Track gasped, dropping to his knees. The heat of the flame in the confined space of the passageway suddenly robbed him of oxygen and seared his face.

There was no choice either—die from the next burst of the flamethrower or die because it exploded if he fired back.

Acting on pure instinct, he triggered both pistols simultaneously toward the man using the flamethrower. A tremendous roar hurled down the passage. The beast had been hit. He threw himself flat to the floor of the passage, and felt the blistering heat as it cooked the air around him. He shielded his head with his hands, and the orange light of fire pushed its way through his closed eyelids.

He could smell nothing but burning gasoline as the metal corridor was transformed into a furnace. He pushed himself up, his guns back in his hands, and stumbled back down the hall, not daring to breathe again.

He reached the base of the metal steps, threw himself against the treads, and crawled upward out of the inferno. His lungs were burning, and the skin on his face was drawn taught where the intense heat had sucked out the moisture.

He wanted desperately to draw a breath, but he knew if he did he would breathe in death. Summoning up all his strength, he lunged for the opening above him.

Track staggered to the deck of the superstructure, gulping in the cool air. A wall of flames sealed the passageway behind him as he looked back.

Track started to his feet. If Desiree were down there he had to get to her. Ramming both pistols into his belt, he started for the metal treads.

Suddenly, Track felt a firm hand on his right shoulder. "What are you doing?" a voice rasped.

It was Baslovitch and he shook the man off. "Going for Desiree," Track almost shouted. "Get the hell out of my way!"

"They're carrying naptha," Baslovitch pleaded. "In

a few minutes this ship will be gone. We have to get away!''

"You get away—" and Track shook Baslovitch's hand from his shoulder.

Baslovitch was hauling at him, trying to pull him away from the steps—away from Desiree. Track's right fist punched out for Baslovitch's face. He missed, and clipped the Russian on the right ear, but Baslovitch didn't let go.

Track leaned over him, hammering his left fist into the Russian's abdomen.

Baslovitch fell back, and as Track ran for the steps, he heard Baslovitch shout, "If she's in there, she's dead, Dan!"

Punctuating the Russian's words, a fireball belched upward. Track reeled back, falling to the deck from the sudden explosion of heat.

Baslovitch was shouting over the roar of the flames, "She's dead if she's down there. We will be too if we don't get off this damn ship!"

"I love her, damn you!" Track yelled at Baslovitch. "I thought I'd lost her on that Greek island, and I'm sure not going to lose her now."

He was on his knees, ramming one of the speed-loaders against the L-Frame's open cylinder.

He slammed the gun closed and leveled it at Baslovitch. "You get out," he stormed. "I'm finding Desiree!"

For a moment, Baslovitch only stared at him. Then he pleaded, "A chopper is coming to pick us off—the damn ship's ready to blow!"

Track cocked the hammer of the L-Frame. It was mechanically unnecessary, but made a wonderful stress mark for an argument. "Bullshit!" he grunted.

A voice was screaming from beyond the superstructure, from the main deck below.

The words were in Russian. "Wait," Baslovitch commanded, and he was up and running to the railing. He shouted down, as Track waited for the fireball to burn itself out. He would have to try this passage. There was time for nothing else. But he sensed it was useless. He started forward, but the chemical smell hit him in the face like a fist.

Suddenly, Baslovitch's voice was behind him. "Track, they have the captain. They found out where Krieger went. And Desiree was taken off the ship, I swear it. She's not here!"

Track wheeled, still holding the cocked pistol. "What if you're lying?" he snarled. His voice was menacing.

Baslovitch's face cracked with a grin. "To save your life—I would lie for that? You must trust me, you have no choice. Go in there and die or trust me and live to find her."

Track licked his lips. His mouth was as dry as cotton.

He lowered the hammer of the L-Frame and lowered his head. "All right," he hissed.

## 18

With the cooperation of the Greek and Albanian governments, Track and Baslovitch had been able to return to Athens, and legally so with their weapons. There they discovered that KGB personnel in Morocco had confirmed the landing of the helicopter, which the captain of the East German freighter had indicated Krieger had used for his escape. At the desert airport where the helicopter had landed, the Lear jet that had taken Krieger from the airport had been made by registration number. It was assumed that the registration number was spurious, but it would be difficult to change the number in midair (though this too could be done with special chemical paints). When they arrived, a massive search by Free World Nations, the Consortium and the KGB and its satellite secret services was already underway to determine the Lear jet's eventual landing site.

As they waited for intelligence to filter through, they set up an operations base in the house owned by the Consortium just outside Athens.

Track sat on the veranda beside the pool, smoking a cigar. Baslovitch sat nearby, reading an American thriller novel. As Track watched the KGB major he smiled, suspecting that somehow the Russian wouldn't be satisfied with the ending—the American antiterrorist would win and the Soviet-sponsored terrorist group he fought would lose.

Track looked back to his copy of *Combat Handguns Magazine*, blindly searching for his drink as he read an article dealing with the .45 ACP. He couldn't find the drink, so he looked up for it. George sat in an inflated chair in the pool, reading as well. Track squinted against the sunlight—it was Ruth Benedict's *Patterns Of Culture*. Track returned to his gun article.

Reading, or perhaps playing chess, was the only way to pass the time. They were waiting. A plane was on alert at the Athens airport, a helicopter on the far side of the estate ready to transport them there. Their weapons and gear were already packed in the back of the little 190 series Mercedes.

Sir Abner Chesterton manned the telephones, alternately waiting for information to be called in and calling out to hunt it down. In the stillness, Track could periodically hear Chesterton's voice.

Track flipped through to another article. He inhaled on his cigar. He waited.

Desiree had been taken aboard a seaplane, but the captain of the freighter had sworn he had not known the destination. Track felt his brow crease into furrows. What would Johannes Krieger do with her? he wondered. He closed his magazine, and sipped at his drink. He knew what he would do with Johannes Krieger when he found him someday. Kill him. No court, no appeals. Krieger could never be allowed the possibility of freedom, the possibility of atrocity again.

Dan Track waited.

HIS NAZI CONTACT HAD DRIVEN in silence through Warsaw and the outlying countryside, saying nothing except at the various checkpoints between city and country. Recalling his geography, Krieger determined that ahead would be the Bug River. There was a Soviet air base there and that was his goal. But first the house, the change of clothes from his disguise as a British businessman. It was a versatile disguise. Removing the mustache and brushing the hair forward over his face, he matched the Canadian passport photo and a new identity.

This next disguise would not be so versatile, but vastly more useful.

The Volkswagen Beetle turned a sharp right up a driveway barely wide enough for one full-sized car to pass without bruising the trees that lined the sides of the road. The noise of gravel crunching under the tires made him realize the VW was stopping—the silent Nazi had been a faultless driver.

Krieger turned to the man. "You drive very well," he said in English.

The man only nodded and stepped out of the car.

Krieger stepped out as well, and stretched his long legs, feeling the blood flow once again into cramped muscles and joints. A long ride in a small car was not his idea of comfort.

The silent Nazi had opened the trunk at the front of the car and was setting down the single suitcase Krieger had brought with him. Krieger looked at the low front porch of the home as a tall, gaunt man with a heavy mustache wearing a turtleneck sweater and the uniform pants of a Soviet officer stepped down from the last of three steps, his feet making a crunching sound across the gravel. The man did not smile, merely walked ahead and stopped, saying, "Herr Krieger, it is a pleasure to meet you."

Krieger nodded. It was always a pleasure for someone to meet him. The man's English was bad, but Major Vassily Krienko spoke no German and Krieger had no desire to bother with Russian. "The pleasure is mine, Major Krienko," he replied.

Krienko's eyes flickered toward the Volkswagen, then Krienko snapped, "That is all, Zbigniev."

Krieger glanced toward the silent Nazi, watching as the man bowed slightly then started to get back into his car.

"Come into my house, please, Herr Krieger," said Krienko.

"Thank you," Krieger nodded. He followed the Soviet air force major up the three steps and across the porch. Krienko held the door open deferentially, and Krieger passed through. It was a comfortable if slightly sparse-looking home, Krieger noted as a woman appeared in the passageway at the far end of what he assumed was a dining room. She was wringing a floral print apron in her hands.

"That is my wife, Herr Krieger," explained Krienko.

"Madame Krienko," Krieger nodded, smiling. The woman curtsied and turned on her heel and disappeared.

Krieger turned to Krienko. "All is in readiness." It was a statement, not a question.

"The MiG-25 is ready, Herr Krieger," responded the Russian. "But it is very fast. You can. . . ."

"I can fly it." Krieger quickly interrupted. "And the bomb is ready and located aboard the aircraft." Again a statement.

"Yes, Herr Krieger. If I should be found out. . ." Krienko faltered.

"You will not be unless it is by your own hand or your own fear," stated Krieger, his voice flat and firm. "The uniform is ready as I requested?"

"Yes, Herr Krieger," Krienko nodded, his face sweating profusely.

"Excellent," said Krieger, who smiled as he patted the major on the back. He had decided now that after he changed identities he would have to kill the major and his wife. The major was too nervous and knew too much and the wife, of course, could tell.

The silent Nazi from the Volkswagen knew nothing.

The wife reappeared, her English, if it were to be believed, worse than her husband's. "A dinner I have made for Herr Krieger, please?'' She said it as a question.

Krieger smiled. ''I am touched by your hospitality, madame, truly touched.'' He was, he thought. Home cooking was always a pleasure, however humble the fare.

''WHERE ARE YOU TAKING ME?''

Whatever voices belonged to those people gripping her upper arms didn't answer her.

''Take this blindfold off,'' demanded Desiree. ''What are you afraid of? My hands are tied behind my back.'' There was no answer. ''Please,'' she swallowed hard. ''I'm feeling sick—those drugs—I need to see. I'm going to throw up.''

There was still no answer, but she felt a change of direction, and the hands started to take her down a staircase. She started to stumble, and was terrified that her anonymous jailers would just let her fall. But the hands only dug into her upper arms more tightly. ''If it's money you want, I've got more money than Johannes Krieger could count. Release me and I'll make you wealthy, wealthy beyond your dreams.'' It was a gambit right out of the movies. But sometimes it actually worked.

Suddenly, the hands stopped her. She felt herself tensing. She'd be true to her words if they released her. Money was something she had in great amounts, something she could always replace or replenish. ''Will you release me?'' she pleaded. ''I'll give you more money than you ever dreamed of having—please.''

When the voice finally came, it carried with it a heavy drawl, like it belonged to someone from the southern United States. ''Could I get into your pants, too?''

She nodded and said, ''If you'll release me, you can have me and the money—but release me first.''

"Would you do anything I want?" the voice asked her.

She hesitated, then complied again. "Yes, anything you want. I swear it if you'll let me go."

"How about the other guy here?" asked the voice.

She felt the muscles around her eyes tightening as she nodded. "Yes—anything he wants, too. Just let me go, please."

She felt the hands on her arms turn her around, felt her naked breasts brush against the rough jacket of the man who had spoken. She felt herself pressed against the man, his clothing scratching the skin of her chest.

"After Johannes Krieger has his ultimate triumph I'll be one of the elite," he snorted, "one of the masters. Maybe then, if you're a good little girl, I'll keep you, let you shine my boots maybe, let you. . . ."

She spit in his face, at least she hoped she hit his face. She felt the rush of air against her left cheek before she felt the pressure of his hand. She tried to turn away, but the impact caught her and stunned her. She collapsed, her body limp in the man's arms, the salty taste of blood on her lips.

She heard a key turn in a lock, and the sound of rusty hinges being worked. She felt herself being hauled erect and turned to her right, then hands on her shoulders, roughly shoving her. She tried making her bare feet move fast enough, felt herself falling, her knees paining her as they scraped against some hard surface. She fell forward, her right cheek thudding into the hard floor, her nose suddenly feeling stiff and sore. She felt tears well up in her eyes, and heard the rusty-sounding hinges again, and the turning of the key in the lock. She lay there, crying, thanking God they hadn't done something worse to her, raped her. Yet.

Desiree twisted her body, trying to get up. At least her ankles weren't bound. The blindfold was wet with her tears. As she tried to move, she felt a wave of nausea pass over her, racking her body. She fell forward again, letting it come. Then in her dark world she rolled over onto her left side, breathing hard. She could smell her own vomit, and it made her head swim. She tried to lift her head but she fell back, her brain swirling, and she lost consciousness.

When she woke up, she tried to open her eyes, then remembered the blindfold. It was sodden. A horrible stench assailed her nose. "Help me!" She screamed the words and her throat burned.

She could tell direction from the source of the acrid smell, and she pushed herself across the floor. It felt like dirt beneath her. She kept moving, tentatively and slowly, pushing her feet in front of her body, exploring the way. Her feet smacked against something hard, and she felt rough concrete against her skin.

She edged her head closer and started to rub the blindfold against the wall, trying to shift it. The concrete sliced away at her skin like a hundred tiny knives. Finally, she could squint and see light with her left eye, the blindfold only down far enough to increase her discomfiture. She kept rubbing at it, getting it down now by wriggling her nose as well. Her nose was still stiff and felt clotted with blood.

Her eyes clamped shut against the light. The blindfold had fallen across her nose, making it hard for her to breathe.

The first thing she saw was the wall. It was gray concrete, streaked with her own blood where she had scraped at the blindfold.

She licked her lips. They felt puffed and swollen, the skin cracked and dry.

She looked down at herself. She was scraped and scratched and naked. But everything looked okay.

She cocked her head back against the wall. The knot

of the blindfold was bound into her hair and it hurt. She studied her prison. It was a cellar, empty except for the puddle of vomit on the floor near the heavy-looking wooden door.

Desiree Goth twisted her body around against the wall, trying to gain leverage against it to stand.

As she stood, more of the nausea swept over her. She closed her eyes until it passed.

Her legs worked, and she slowly started across the room toward the solitary barred window. The glass was dirty and she couldn't see clearly through it. By standing on her tiptoes, she was able to reach the bottom of the glass panel with her face. The blindfold was still over her nose and she rubbed it against the window by moving her face back and forth. The dirt was old and hardened, but a clear spot started to emerge.

Leaning against the wall, cold against her flesh, she peered through the eyehole in the streaky dirt. Staring back at her was a chicken.

## 19

Entering the air base had been easier than he had anticipated. Major Krienko had done his work well—the late Major Krienko, Krieger smiled. He walked toward the hangar, looking smart, he thought, in his blue Soviet major's uniform.

His lapels bore both the insignia of the KGB and crossed wings, but the former was the most important element of his dual identity. He casually returned an enlisted man's salute and entered the hangar. A mechanic stood beneath the fuselage of his plane, making a final pre-flight check. As he drew closer to the MiG-25, passing on an angle from the tip of its starboard wing, he could read the aircraft number painted on the fuselage. The number ninety-two was in blood red, but not bordered in white like the red star on the tail. A strip of dark gray paint lined the top of the sand-colored fuselage, reaching from the drab olive-colored nose cone back and around the pilot's canopy.

The mechanic, a sergeant, snapped to attention as he approached. In Russian, the man said, "Comrade Major Gerovin, your aircraft awaits!"

Krieger only noded, walking closer to the machine. It would do near Mach 3, perhaps vastly better than that. An SR-71 could catch it and pass it. But it was among the fastest of military aircraft.

An officer was approaching, and Krieger eyed the man, placing the rank subordinate to him. He returned the young captain's salute, the man saying, "Comrade

Major Gerovin, I have been instructed to inspect your orders prior to take-off.''

Krieger smiled as he reached under his tunic and produced the documents. They were marked in Russian, Soviet Air Force, Fighter Aviation/Air Defense Command, National Air Defense Command. They were signed by the Marshal of Aviation and countersigned by the head of the Committee for State Security. Krieger couldn't restrain a smile as he watched the young officer's eyes widen.

The captain returned the orders, saluting. "I did not know, comrade major—" he began.

"You were not supposed to know," Krieger cut him off. "All is in readiness?"

"Yes, comrade major."

"I shall change then into my flight suit. Have it brought from my car. It is parked outside the hangar." Krieger glanced at his watch, a Rolex GMT which went better with his image. "I wish to be airborne in exactly seventeen minutes."

"Yes, comrade major. Sergeant—the automobile!" he snapped at the mechanic.

Krieger smiled, and fished his keys from his trouser pocket. He called after the sergeant as he jogged off, "Sergeant, you might need these!" He tossed the keys to the mechanic.

Soon he would be inside Russia, flying over the breadth of the nation that was one of the two most powerful on earth—one of the vultures that had picked at the bones of the Reich. And soon the thermonuclear device that Klaus Gurnheim had so meticulously prepared would do its work.

He clapped his hands together softly, rubbing them like a man would do if he were cold. "I shall change now," he proclaimed, starting across the hangar. The young captain was at his heels.

SIR ABNER CHESTERTON ran across the marbled floor of the corridor, Track watching him from the leather easy chair beside the cold hearth of the library. Track got to his feet, looking at his drink for a moment. There was something in the way Chesterton ran, in the look on his face as well. Track set his drink down.

"George, I think we've got something, George...." He walked to his nephew's chair, and nudged the younger man's right shoulder to awaken him. Miles Jefferson, who had joined them earlier, started to sit up. He too had been dozing.

"Wake up, George, come on," Track prodded.

"Marvin, jeez," George muttered.

"You're dreaming about when you were a nuclear guard," Track said firmly, and he watched as George's eyes suddenly opened.

"Stay awake," he added, walking across the room to the open sliding doors. Sir Abner was nearly through the corridor, slowing his run, smiling.

"You've got something?" Track said.

Breathless, Chesterton began. "A lead, we've got a lead. Baslovitch is on the telephone now. He had come in to talk for a moment and the telephone rang. It was the KGB in Warsaw. One of their men had infiltrated the Nazi underground, and just did some driving for them. He took a tall, British-looking man to the home of an air force major, a Major Krienko. The man matched the description the freighter captain was persuaded to give.

"The KGB man left, but waited in the woods with binoculars. Krienko never came out, nor did his wife. But a third person did, dressed as an air force major with insignia designating him as KGB. He drove off in a car that the driver had never seen, presumably Krienko's. The driver waited two hours, but after seeing no movement he went down to Krienko's house and peered through a window. He admitted that he threw up. Krienko's wife was in the kitchen, her throat slit. The driver broke down the door and ran inside. Krienko was dead as well and there was no sign of Krieger. The driver tried using the telephone, but the wires had been cut and the vibrator in the mouthpiece removed. He ran back to his car and then raced back to Warsaw to report his findings. The man dressed as the air force KGB major had been gone more than four hours by then."

"Shit," Track snapped.

"Yes, quite," Chesterton agreed. "Baslovitch is trying to get through KGB red tape—I don't envy the man—to get permission to contact the Soviet Air Force. The KGB thinks Krieger may be a mysterious Major Gerovin, who flew off in an MiG-25, but the air force base won't designate where."

"If Krieger went to the trouble of stealing a plane and killing the Nazis who set it up, he'll have one of the nuclear devices aboard," Track ventured. He heard Miles Jefferson make a low whistle.

"If he drops one over Russia," Miles began. He left the conclusion open for speculation.

"But the MiG-25 isn't a bomber," Chesterton stated.

"And if he didn't have the right altitude," Track heard George say, "the electromagnetic pulse from the detonation would put his plane out of commission."

"The Russians use vacuum tubes in their aircraft," Track reminded him, "not like us. Vacuum tubes are less susceptible to electromagnetic pulse."

"Great," George whispered.

"My God! An air burst over Moscow perhaps," Chesterton mused.

Track was studying his shoes, thinking. He heard the distant clicking of heels on the marble floor of the corridor and looked up. Baslovitch was running quickly toward them.

The KGB man shouted, ''He's heading to the capital of Siberia—and may be there by now. And there was an item aboard the plane. It may be a nuclear device.''

Track started to run for the front door, shouting to Chesterton, ''Get on the horn, Sir Abner, get the clearances set up to get us into the Soviet Union and get the jet revved up at the airfield.''

''I'm comin' along,'' Track heard George shouting.

''You and Miles look for Desiree,'' ordered Track. ''We might have to kill Krieger to stop him, so it's up to you to find Desiree.''

Track punched the double front doors open, almost shattering the stained glass as he raced out of the house. Across the lawn was the chopper. He shouted ahead to the pilot sitting on the grass beside it. ''Charlie, get the engines going, pronto, hurry!'' Track felt it in his blood. It was Krieger. Krieger had a bomb. Krieger would use it and maybe start World War III just for fun.

Charlie was climbing into the cockpit. Behind him, Track heard someone getting the Mercedes rolling. The weapons were in the car's trunk and would have to be transferred to the chopper.

He kept running for the machine.

## 20

Krieger rammed his gloved hands into the pockets of his gray overcoat, thankful for the warmth. The weather in Novosibirsk was not at all to his liking, he reflected, but Siberia wasn't thought of as a vacation spot, except by Siberians. The air was clear and clean and he liked that. A light snow was falling, the wind tracking it into lines across the gray tarmac of the runway.

He looked skyward. Soon it would snow heavily. When the detonation took place, the snow would become radioactive and wherever it fell it would bring a blanket of white crystaline death. He smiled at the thought. It was all working out better than he had hoped.

He watched as the technicians unloaded the crate from the MiG, then carefully transferred it to the van. "Be careful with that," he urged in Russian, "or there will be serious repercussions."

It was, after all, a thermonuclear device.

The air force personnel were nearly through loading it. He started toward the van, watching with mild interest as the device was secured inside. The last of the loading crew jumped out to the runway surface and nearly lost his balance. Krieger reached out to support the man at his elbow. "Thank you, comrade major," the young man nodded.

Krieger flashed a smile. He turned and addressed the man heading the work crew. "Corporal, as your officer instructed you, this is of the highest priority. Tell no one

of what you have seen here, no one of even any slight
suspicion you might have as to the contents of this con-
tainer,'' he said as he gestured inside the van. ''The continued security of the Soviet Union, of the very loved
ones whom you represent in uniform, is at stake. Suffice
to say, this involves the foiling of an American capitalist
plot against the workers of the Soviet Union. I have told
you and your men more than I should have, but trust in
our loyal comrades is something of which the Soviet
people shall never be deprived by the forces that would
destroy us.''

He watched the glow of pride in the corporal's eyes,
the straightening of the shoulders of the men of the
work crew.

''I salute you,'' Krieger said and he did.

The corporal closed the van doors and Krieger walked
toward the driver's door.

He boarded the van and gunned the engine to life. He
turned on the windshield wipers, the snow was falling
more heavily now and it was more than a fifteen-mile
drive to Academgorodok and the cream of Soviet in tel-
ligentsia.

And his destiny.

THE KNOWLEDGE THAT he was flying in an American
business jet across the Soviet Union gave Track the
chills. They had stopped to refuel in Chelyabinsk and
had gotten airborne again almost immediately. Baslovitch was continually on the radio, conferring with his
KGB superiors, air force personnel, the Aviation Marshal's office and the Kremlin. Baslovitch had agreed
that to intercept Krieger would result in one of two
possible occurrences—Krieger would change identity
and set the nuclear device for remote detonation; or, if
Krieger were unable to escape, he would simply
detonate the device and possibly issue some low fre-

quency radio signal to have the other ninety-eight detonated.

The potential end of civilization was not a cheery prospect.

Track wore his .357 and the Trapper .45 but took no comfort in them. On the ground beneath him were millions of Russians who had been taught for decades to hate what he stood for. He touched the flame from his Zippo to a cigar, and continued to watch. They were crossing over a river and it was broad and gunmetal gray. White snow capped the high mountains on the distant horizon.

"You look nervous, my friend," came Baslovitch's voice, interrupting his thoughts.

Track looked up from his seat. "I am nervous."

"About Krieger?" asked Baslovitch.

"Nervousness won't help that," responded Track, taking a pull at his cigar.

"Then about flying over the Soviet Union?" Baslovitch wondered.

"Yes," said Track, "perhaps a little nervous about that."

"You are here as our ally, our invited guest," said Baslovitch in a magnanimous tone.

Track dismissed that, asking instead, "Will they go along with waiting?"

"The head of my section in KGB is indisposed, fortunately for us. I have been in direct contact with his superior. Unless the situation should change, we are given permission to endeavor to apprehend Krieger in our own way. As of yet, it has been unconfirmed that he has landed. Apparently his counterfeit orders are so good in appearance that they are being obeyed, and superceding their security restrictions is difficult."

"The police-state policies come home to roost, huh," Track said, smiling.

Baslovitch only shrugged, "Perhaps, but it is police-state efficiency that will undo Krieger as well."

"What about the device—if we stop him in time?" Track urged.

"It will stay in the Soviet Union until arrangements can be made to return it to your country, if indeed such arrangements can be negotiated. It is, after all, a lapse in your nation's security that originally allowed this terrorist Krieger to take possession of this and the other devices."

Track looked at Baslovitch, saying nothing. The cold war was getting very chilly, he thought.

SHE HEARD HIM OPENING the door, heard his patronizing voice. "Remember, honey, if you've worked off that blindfold again, I'm gonna make you eat this stuff with your hands tied behind your back, make you lick it out of your bowl like a dog."

She smiled. She had worked her hands loose, after they had been tied again, this time in front of her, following the scraps of food she had been given that morning. No effort had been made to clean or even disguise the smell of the vomit that choked the room. She had been given no clothes to wear, and no plumbing, not even a bucket, had been provided for her use. She had resorted to making catholes in the earthen floor with her toes and covering them with dirt, which she kicked in place.

She hated.

She waited.

The man who had brought her breakfast had secured the blindfold after tying her once more. He hadn't even seemed concerned that she had worked it free.

She hated him more for that.

He had worn a pistol on his belt, a Smith & Wesson stainless steel K-Frame with a four-inch barrel, probably a .357. She had to get the gun.

She waited, wishing she had mastered karate or some other martial art. He passed through the doorway. "You behind that door waitin' for me, huh?" he said. There was a mocking tone in his voice.

She was indeed, but hanging from the hook on the inside of the door instead, this giving her a foot's height advantage. As he came around the door, she dropped the noose of rope that had bound her hands over his head, around his neck, with the rope looped over the hook, she threw her weight down to the floor, the other end of the rope secured around her waist. It was a one-shot try. She had to break the man's neck with the weight of her body.

She hurtled herself downward, suspended in midair a moment at the level of the backs of his knees.

Then she heard the loud crack, like the breaking of an enormous wishbone. She fell the rest of the way to the floor, shielding her head with her arms and hands. His body fell on top of her.

All the breath was forced out of her body. Coughing, she dragged herself from under his body. She remembered to undo the knotted rope around her waist—her ribs ached.

She crawled away from him, staring at him for an instant. His eyes were wide open. She'd seen death before, caused its occurrence more than once.

This was death.

She crawled back toward him, reaching to the police-type holster on his trouser belt.

She had the gun in her hands. She read the barrel legend—it was a .357 Magnum.

She stood up, and moved cautiously toward the door. There was no sound, no sign of alarm. She went back to the dead man, her persecutor. She felt through his pockets, finding speed-loaders for the revolver armed with .38 caliber lead hollow points. That was all the better—she hadn't relished the idea of firing full house .357s with so light a gun. She checked the cylinder. There were .38s there, too.

She stripped the man of his shirt, and draped it over her naked and bruised body. After a final look around her prison cell she walked through the doorway. She locked the door behind her, and threw the key down the dirt-floored corridor. Clutching the stainless Smith & Wesson, she started to climb the basement stairs. There was a sound ahead of her, a television set, she guessed. She stopped beneath an open trap door. Slowly, holding the gun more tightly than she had ever held her lover Dan Track, she peered over the floorboards through the opening.

The head of a man was visible above the back of an easy chair. There was a children's cartoon program on the television and the man was laughing at it. Slowly, she climbed the last of the steps, silently praying that a board didn't creak. As she stepped through the opening and onto the rolled-back rug, she looked about the room. There was only the man in the chair. Two men's coats were visible hanging from a hall tree down a hallway.

She would gamble.

One of the cartoon characters fired a gun at the head of another. The second character's head turned black and the hair burned away. In the next scene the character who had been shot in the head was chasing the other one.

Real life was different. At ten feet, unless there was something fundamentally wrong with the revolver, she couldn't miss. She raised the revolver, and double actioned it toward the rear of the man's head.

The top of his head blew away, and blood and brains smeared all over the color screen.

She held her breath. There were no shouts, no alarms, no screams, nothing.

She was alone in the house with two men dead of her own hand.

She stood there a moment, watching the cartoons. It ended, and a short titles segment followed, then the screen went blank for an instant. Call letters were flashed and an announcer's voice intoned, "The big one to watch in Springfield, Illinois."

"Springfield, Illinois," she repeated. She had heard of the city. It was in south central Illinois, she remembered.

Desiree Goth walked across the room, and stared through the front window. A station wagon was parked in the yard, and chickens and ducks wandered about. Fields covered in snow filled her view. She took a deep breath and forced herself to explore the dead man's pockets. She found car keys that read, Ford Family of Fine Cars. She continued the search, and found a folding knife. She left it closed. Her nails were damaged enough. The pockets also held loose ammunition, .38 Specials. On the coffee table, beside the partially headless body, was a revolver, a Colt detective special.

A gun in each hand, Desiree Goth explored the house. There were no women's clothes, only the belongings of the two men.

But there was a bathroom. It was a risk, but there were towels and there was even shampoo. It was one of the ones high in detergent, but her hair needed the cleaning.

Desiree looked down at the stainless steel pistol and shrugged. She set the gun in the shower stall and turned on the water. When the temperature was right, she stripped off the shirt and stepped inside, leaving the other gun on the sink. She turned up the water.

She had seen something in her eyes in the bathroom mirror, something she was happy to see. Despite the dirt, the unkempt hair, the smell of her flesh, there was the spark of strength and humanity.

They hadn't taken that from her. As she soaped her body, she watched the shiny, wet revolver. It reassured her, but not more than her will reassured her.

## 21

Twenty-four thousand people lived in Academgoro-dok—Academic City. Science City it was sometimes called. The cream of Soviet medical, computer, geological, agricultural and less widely known disciplines resided there, freely exchanging ideas on science and technology. The winners of the prestigious scientific prizes, three thousand of the best research minds, also called Academgorodok home.

Johannes Krieger stood before fifty of the finest minds now, summoned here for him in the little scientific community on the edge of the reservoir.

Before him on a laboratory table was the bomb. He began to speak. "This weapon was smuggled into the Soviet Union with the express intention of destroying a vital segment of Soviet society, the intention of crippling the Soviet Union irreparably." The truth almost always sounded convincing. But his next remarks diverged from it. "It is an American secret weapon, sent to destroy us, I alone have been charged to bring this weapon here, to you—the finest minds available for the task. You, Paprovitch," he said as he looked at a lean-faced, almost sorrowful-looking bearded man wearing a white lab coat, "you were once principal-weapons designer for the Soviet Union."

"My research has taken me elsewhere, away from destruction," said the scientist.

"But your skills are still the best," Krieger went on forcefully. "You will hand pick a team to assist you in dismantling the weapon before it can be detonated. I have ordered the city sealed and the research complex here closed. No one is to be admitted without my express permission. Nor is anyone to be allowed to leave. Some members of the KGB are themselves suspect of complicity with the American imperialists.'' He held a folded section of lined paper from a pocket notebook high in the air for all to see. "On this slip of paper is the telephone number of operation headquarters. Once you have defused the American weapon of mass destruction, you are to call this number, Paprovitch. Not before. The switchboard has been ordered closed here until you make this call. No incoming or outgoing calls will be allowed. Revisionist elements are everywhere, I fear.''

"But surely we must know something about the nature of this device before we can begin.'' It was a woman who spoke, and Krieger guessed she belonged to Paprovitch.

"Madame,'' he replied, and again he elected the truth, "it is comprised of 500-kilotons, that is its effective yield. I am certain the designer of this instrument arranged detonation to be impossible to avoid. It will trigger if the slightest mistake is made. Yours is an impossible task—but it must be accomplished.''

"Why was this weapon, this horrible thing, not brought to a bomb-disposal area, or detonated in some safe location?'' asked a dignified-looking white-haired man. He smoked a pipe, and the tobacco smelled very good.

"There are, doctor, ninety-eight other devices similar to this one,'' Krieger replied. "Circumstances may arise in which more of these will be set against the Soviet Union. For that purpose, this device must be defused rather than detonated.''

The woman spoke again. "There are ninety-eight more of these—500-kilotons each?'' She sounded incredulous.

"Many of these are already in Europe," Krieger went on, "waiting to be set against important cities and installations. It is imperative that you do what you must do." He glanced at his watch and continued, his voice marked with urgency. "There is one further reason why it was brought here and you were not transported to some safer sight. Time is critical. In thirty-two minutes and ten seconds, if you cannot disarm it, it will detonate of its own accord." There were cries and gasps. One woman screamed. He saw tears in the eyes of the bearded man, Paprovitch.

"I salute you," he said, "and now I must take my leave." He handed the piece of paper with the phone number written across it to Paprovitch, turned and walked briskly from the room.

He listened to is own heels clicking on the laboratory floor. He was immensely pleased with himself. But as the laboratory doors—steel, triple thickness armor-plated steel—slammed closed with a pneumatic hiss in his wake, he could feel that the KGB was closing in, and perhaps the American Dan Track as well. He smiled—it was time to change identities.

"I AM SORRY, MAJOR," the base commander said in English, Track doubly appreciating the courtesy because of the awkwardness with which the man handled the language. "But the orders of Major Gerovin take precedence over your own. I witnessed these myself. It is not a breach of security to admit that they were cosigned by the aviation marshal and the director of your own organization."

"Those were forged orders, comrade colonel," Baslovitch said politely.

"I have only your word for this, major, and please believe I mean no disrespect," the colonel smiled. Track felt cold as snow drifted down past the upturned collar of his bomber jacket, then melted on his neck.

Baslovitch shrugged his shoulders. "I regret having to show you these additional orders, then, comrade colonel." Track held back the smile—he had learned where Baslovitch carried his pistol.

The H&K P7 appeared in Baslovitch's right fist, and the sound of the squeeze cocker being activated was loud in the artificial stillness the snow imparted. The muzzle of the pistol was pointed at the colonel's face. "Back my play, Dan," Baslovitch grunted.

Track had the Metalife Custom L-Frame already in his right fist, aimed toward the knot of junior officers standing some paces away. "You got it," he replied.

"Major—you overstep your authority," challenged the base commander.

"I am KGB," Baslovitch said severely. "My authority supercedes yours, colonel. Do you like this part of Siberia? There are other spots not so pleasant or as lovely as Novosibirsk, believe me. I'll kill you if I have to. This man you aided is a Nazi named Johannes Krieger. He carries with him a nuclear device with a 500-kiloton yield. He is a mass murderer. He is here to detonate this device and destroy the entire city, killing thousands. The river will carry radiation everywhere throughout its course. Millions will be effected. You must tell me now, or do you gradually wish to die?"

When the Russian colonel gave no response, Track shrugged, and shifted the L-Frame to his left fist. With his free hand he drew out the Trapper Scorpion, thumb-cocking the little .45. He began to speak. He was cold, tired and angry. "Sergei, you have a fundamental failing—you don't use psychology in dealing with people." While Baslovitch watched, Track rammed the muzzle of the .45 against the base commander's crotch. He looked the colonel in the eye. "Tell Baslovitch what he needs to know in ten seconds or I blow your testicles off one at a time. One...two...three...four...."

SOUND PSYCHOLOGICAL PRINCIPLES and reason had prevailed, Track realized. They walked hurriedly now across the airfield to the hangar in which Krieger's MiG-25 was stored. As they entered the hangar, Baslovitch took from his coat a device about the size of a transistor radio and jacked an earphone cable into its side.

They stopped before the sand-colored MiG-25. Track still held both pistols, one trained on a group of officers and men gathering behind them, and the other, the .45, on the base commander. He flickered his eyes from the men he guarded to Baslovitch—he was sweeping the radio-like device over the open cargo hatch of the MiG-25.

The KGB man turned around, pulling the earplug from his ear. "This is a radiation detection device," Baslovitch announced. "There is evidence of residual radiation in the cargo area. You, the officer there," he said, pointing to a man who looked little more than twelve years old, even his hat too big for him. Track reflected that every army sent its quartermasters to the same tailoring school—if it's not so big that it falls off, it fits. "Come here, now!" Baslovitch ordered.

The young officer walked forward and stopped less than a yard from Baslovitch. "Now, lieutenant. You will place this earphone in or by your ear—whichever ear you normally hold against a telephone will do the best. Then sweep the instrument along the open cargo. Announce what your results are."

The young man nodded, holding the earpiece behind his left ear, the radio-like device in his right hand. He swept it over the open cargo hatch, inside the fuselage, then stopped. He returned the device to Baslovitch. Track watched the man's Adam's apple bob nervously, the shoulders thrown back. "The major is correct, there is radiation. We have apparently transferred a nuclear device."

The base commander suddenly decided to ignore Track's .45, and started forward. Track did nothing to stop him. The colonel stopped midway between Track and Baslovitch and the young lieutenant. "I was wrong," the commander said simply. He turned and saluted Baslovitch. "We are at your disposal—my men, all of us, to stop this terrorist. If you are somehow deceiving me, I shall kill you with my bare hands. But I cannot afford the risk to the people of this region. What do you want us to do?"

Baslovitch nodded toward Track. "This American has fought against Johannes Krieger before. He is in charge of the operation until the actual device is retrieved."

Track watched as all eyes turned to him. "If he's masquerading as KGB and his orders look that good," said Track, "he'll probably have turned what police or military are available, wherever he's gone against us. It may mean fighting your own people," he added. "I'm an antiCommunist. But I can empathize, I can sympathize with what words like these would mean. No one wants to kill his own," and Track smiled as he said the words, "his own comrades."

TRACK CEASED BOTHERING to count the number of telephone calls that followed. At last, word came through that Academgorodok had been closed to motorized traffic going in or out, and the actual scientific institute was sealed and ringed by KGB personnel and police from the area.

The base commander set down the telephone. The steam heat of the office was stifling as he spoke. "The most brilliant minds of the Soviet Union are there," he explained to Track. "There is also a boarding school for the most brilliant of children, those with the most promising intellects. My son, he is there. My first sergeant's daughter, she is there as a researcher. My wife works in the complex as a research assistant. She was working late tonight.'' The man's face dripped sweat, but not from the heat of the office, Track realized. ''And our van which this Krieger requisitioned, was seen to enter the institute complex.''

Track closed his eyes. He suddenly realized what Krieger was doing. ''He spoke of a nuclear device or something that was being brought here, that it was some horrifying American plot.'' Track thought aloud. ''Let's say he keeps to that idea. He brought the bomb to the institute complex. Just to plant it? Why go through more security than he needed?'' Track walked toward the wall map of the area behind the colonel's desk. ''There's a reservoir right at the edge of—how do you say it?''

Baslovitch answered, ''A-ca-dem-gor-o-dok.''

''Academgorodok,'' Track repeated. ''There's a reservoir there. He could have planted the device, come back here and taken off. Or used some other means of quick exit. This is a setup, I'm sure of it. Are any persons at,'' he stumbled over it, then said it slowly, ''Academgorodok who were involved or are involved in your country's thermonuclear weapons program?''

The colonel's eyes flickered to Baslovitch, the KGB man. Track looked at Baslovitch. ''Well?''

''Doctor Yuri Paprovitch,'' Baslovitch replied.

''Isn't he the one who quit the Soviet nuclear weapons program? I remember there was a big stink about it,'' Track said.

''He is a man of peace,'' Baslovitch shrugged.

''Then I know what he's doing,'' Track decided. ''He had Klaus Gurnheim set the nuclear device to be tripped off.''

''What is tripped?'' The colonel looked puzzled.

Baslovitch said something in Russian, and the colonel nodded.

"He's using Paprovitch and some of the others as his detonator. He probably told them he had this horrible American weapon and for some reason or another they were the only ones who could disarm it, and that's why he sealed the institute complex. As they start to dismantle it, they'll detonate it. He likely gave them some sort of time limit to increase the probabilities of them not finding the tripping devices."

"I have helicopters."

Track looked at the base commander. "You come with us—we'll need all the influence we can muster if we want to avoid a shooting war with the people guarding the institute."

"There is a helipad on the roof," the commander said.

Track picked up the SPAS-12 that he'd retrieved from the business jet still parked on the field. Baslovitch stood up. "Shall we, gentlemen?" the Russian nodded.

Track started for the office door.

## 22

The five rotor blades churning through the snowy skies overhead made a terrible racket, Track thought, turning toward Baslovitch as the man tapped him on the shoulder. Baslovitch gestured to their headset and pulled his away, then leaned toward Track's right ear, "To save you trying to memorize details to tell your American CIA, this is a variant of Mil Mi-24—in the West it has the rather peculiar designation of Hind—and this is classified a Hind-A." Track watched as the Russian's eyes lit with a smile. "Maximum cruising speed is 229 miles per hour. Each ship carries four Spirals, it's an advanced type of antitank rocket. Among other things, the stub wings have pods for 128 fifty-seven millimeter rockets."

Track nodded. "I'm not a spy but I do like helicopters—thanks a lot." Besides himself and Baslovitch seated behind the pilot and the copilot—in this case the pilot was the base commander himself—there were eight other men, all heavily armed. Two more helicopters, each with two man instead of four-man crews and thus carrying ten armed personnel, comprised the rest of the fleet. Track glanced at his wristwatch, then out the steamed Plexiglas ahead of him through the pilot's bubble and beyond through the swirling snow. The lights of Academgorodok were coming up fast—at least he assumed these were the lights of Academic City. He found himself silently admiring the Russians. Setting up such a community where the greatest minds could exchange interdisciplinary discoveries was brilliant. The atmosphere in the city would be electric, he thought.

He heard a noise through his headset and remembered to replace it, listening now. "A three-pronged formation, major, is that to your liking—I mean Major Track? Is it?"

"I'm sorry, colonel," Track said into the tiny microphone in front of his lips. "I didn't catch all of that."

"I was referring to strategy here. I will announce over the PA system that the problem exists. We will wait for a signal flare or some arrangement of shots to be fired or a radio contact. We will wait three minutes, hovering. If there is no agreement from the forces on the ground, we will initiate a three-pronged attack. Our craft will land on the institute roof, the craft to starboard on the institute lawn, the third craft on the parking lot. I believe the word is pincher—"

"Pincer," Track corrected.

"Pincer—from both sides, and then ourselves down from the roof," stated the colonel.

"Your men—they realize," Track began.

"They are all volunteers. None of them wishes to kill his own countryman, but all realize the situation. They were told the truth so far as we know it," the colonel continued.

Track nodded, realizing the colonel couldn't see him. "Good. You've got the ball, colonel—until we get on the ground. But tell your people one thing—Krieger could be anyone. If they're looking for a major with an air force uniform and KGB designation, they'll never find him. He could be anyone, from looking like Doctor Paprovitch to the cleaning lady. Anyone."

"Even yourself, Major Track?" and Track heard the colonel's laughter. "We are over the target."

Track heard the words in Russian coming over the PA, echoing to the fenced-in area surrounding the institute. He doubted they would be believed, but regardless of the potential wasting of three minutes, they had to try to convince the defenders of the institute. They had to try. . . .

Three minutes ticked away, and Track watched the sweep second hand of the Rolex pass the inverted triangle that held the place of the twelve—but there was no flare, there was no radio message, there was no triple series of three shots fired in the white swirling darkness below.

He turned toward Baslovitch—tears streamed down the man's face. He heard the colonel's voice, sounding tight, choked. "If you Americans are right and there is a God, then let Him damn this Johannes Krieger who makes us kill our own comrades." There was a long pause, then in Russian a word Track recognized, *"Nachinat."* It translated simply—begin—and Track felt the Hind-A shudder slightly as misiles from each side stub wing were fired toward the ground beyond the police positions into a park. The night below lit with fire and the helicopter was moving.

The craft to starboard broke off, arcing sharply away, veering downward toward the snow covered front lawns of the institute. The craft to port accelerated more rapidly than Track thought possible, climbing, seeming almost to skip over the snow-splotched institute roof, then dropped from sight. Their own helicopter was angling downward, going at a slower speed than either of the other two craft. Track guessed the base commander spent more time flying a desk than a gunship.

Track worked the action of the SPAS-12, chambering a round of buckshot. He was using double "O" Buck exclusively because of the confined shooting situation there would be once inside the building and the desire not to overpenetrate a wall and kill some innocent party. He rammed a fresh round into the magazine tube, bringing capacity to a full eight. The stock was collapsed and he left it that way, again because of the confined battle area he expected.

Baslovitch had an AKM.

Track could feel the helicopter settling, the swirling snow raging about them now in an artificial blizzard. He heard the base commander's voice. "Touchdown in five—one, two, three, four—we've landed."

Track ripped open the safety restraint while one of the eight men—the Soviet equivalent of air police he assumed—slid back the portside doors. He then leapt out, with Baslovitch and the others closer behind him.

A voice shouted out a warning from behind an external air-conditioning unit or heat pump. Track wheeled toward the voice, but gunfire started to crash through the night. Track edged the trigger guard safety forward and worked the SPAS's trigger back, loosing a round of double "O" Buck. Then he was on the run, slipping on the snowy roof, regaining his balance, then firing a second and third round as he dived for cover behind an identical duplicate of the climate-control unit. Assault-rifle fire punctuated the night around him, and the snow swirled wildly in the downdraft of the five rotor blades as the Soviet Air Police advanced in a ragged wedge toward the origin of the gunfire. The PA system from the Hind-A continued to demand surrender, trying to reason with the defenders.

Track was up and running, Baslovitch beside him as they started for what seemed to be a doorway leading down from the roof and inside. Four men raced to block them off, AK-47s firing. Track pumped the SPAS's trigger, the action set for semi-automatic. Baslovitch was firing his AKM. More men joined the original four, making six in all now, all of them going down.

Track reached the door first—it was locked.

"Step back," Baslovitch yelled, turning his face

away. Track did the same, hearing a long, ragged burst from the AKM. Track turned back toward the doorway, half wheeled right, snapping his left foot in a tae kwon-do kick toward the locking mechanism.

The lock fell away, and Baslovitch hammered the wooden stock of the AKM against the door, swinging it partially open on its hinges.

Baslovitch wrenched the door all the way open and sprayed the AKM down the stairway, then stepped back. Track framed the door from the other side, feeding fresh loads of double "O" Buck into the SPAS, chambering a round, then adding one more round to the tube. He had eight again.

"Me first—this is an alley sweeper," Track snapped, his face stinging with the bombardment of snow from the rotor downdraft. He turned into the doorway, firing four rounds fast from the SPAS, then ducked inside, flattening against the wall. He heard Baslovitch's AKM tap out its message, seeing the muzzle flashes in the darkness. Then Baslovitch's feet were on the interior surface. "You ready?" Track snapped.

"Ready," the Russian's voice rasped.

Track nodded in the darkness, feeding four fresh rounds into the SPAS. "Let's go, down the stairs." Track worked the SPAS's trigger, firing four rounds into the blackness of the stairwell. Moans and screams of pain were the only replies. Muzzles flashed like flickering candles in the darkness, bright then extinguished as he raced downward. He felt himself falling, tripping over a body, skidding down the stairs, bracing himself halfway and stopping his fall. He fired the SPAS into the blackness again, then edged downward on his belly. There were no screams, no shouts. There was no answering gunfire.

"Keep your head down." It was Baslovitch, and Track tucked down, a stream of AKM fire pouring over him, muzzle flashes lighting the blackness of the stairwell.

Track shouted, "Cease-fire for a minute." He'd reloaded the magazine tube and was on his feet again, taking the treads more slowly this time. He stopped at the base of the stairwell. He could faintly see the doorway. "Cover me," he shouted hoarsely into the darkness behind him, hearing the sound of Baslovitch changing sticks for the AKM.

"Right," Baslovitch's voice came.

Track tried the door—its knob turned under his hand. It opened outward and he kicked the door open, blinded temporarily by the bright light from the corridor beyond. Gunfire tore through the open doorway toward him, and he tucked back, hearing answering fire from Baslovitch. He stabbed the SPAS-12 around the corner of the doorway, working the trigger three times, then three more times.

"Let's go!" He shouted the words as he dived through, rolling into the corridor, jumping up, emptying the SPAS as his eyes searched for cover.

He ran for a doorway, assault-rifle fire chewing into the floor around his feet, ripping chunks of plaster from the corridor walls. Chunks of ceiling tile crashed down in a stream of dust.

Track hugged into the doorway, reloaded the SPAS, chambered a round, and added an eighth round to the tube. "Sergei," he called, "count to three and run for it, toward the doorway to your right as you make it through!"

"Right," came the reply. "Counting—one—two—THREE!"

Baslovitch broke cover, running, firing the AKM in a sweeping, ragged burst that would empty the magazine. Track covered him, working the SPAS-12 as fast as he could pull the trigger, emptying the Franchi shotgun.

Baslovitch was safe in cover. Track started reloading, one pocket nearly empty of shotgun shells. He glanced at his Rolex—there couldn't be much time left now before the nuclear device would blow.

"Go for it—down the corridor," Track shouted, breaking cover, firing as he ran. Baslovitch was moving, his AKM spitting fire.

YURI PAPROVITCH LOOKED to his dark-haired, dark-eyed wife at his side. "You should have taken the children and left when the major brought the bomb here," he said softly.

"No—the institute was sealed," he heard her whisper, watching her hands. She was a cardiac surgeon, and she was using this touch, this delicacy, to unravel the wires within what appeared to be the main detonator.

"The guards know you, they trust you, they would have perhaps let you leave," he persisted.

Paprovitch shuddered, hearing more of the gunfire from beyond the steel doors of the demonstration laboratory. He watched his wife's eyes flicker each time there was a fresh burst of fire.

He looked from her to his colleague. Anatol's white mane of hair fell across his eyes and he brushed it back as he scrutinized the detonator head. "This is useless," the older man began. "I tell you, Yuri Gestanyik Paprovitch, this is useless. The entire device is set as a trap."

"I think the war has begun already." Paprovitch looked at the origin of the voice, Anatol's daughter, Tatiana. "It is World War III," she said without raising her eyes from the systems diagram she was completing at the drafting table at the far end of the laboratory table.

"It is not a world war," Paprovitch heard his wife reprove. "No one would be stupid enough."

"If the Americans sent this bomb as the major said,

then whatever other reason?'' Dimitri Vassilovitch asked, using a microwave scanner near Anatol by the detonator head. Vassilovitch was a radio astronomer interested in geology as a sideline. ''It must be a world war—we are all doomed anyway. This will likely be a prime target for the Americans, so we can all be killed.''

Paprovitch threw down the tiny jeweler's screwdriver he was using to work at the timer mechanism—he heard a spring pop. ''It is not World War III—we are not all going to die unless we detonate this bomb by accident— I tell you that!''

He swallowed hard, and sighed loudly. His wife's hand touched at his and he looked into her eyes. ''I love you,'' she whispered, then returned to her work.

He returned to his, hearing young Tatiana. She was only nineteen and already held a doctorate and was working toward a second. ''From this diagram I make, I can see the arrangement clearly enough,'' she said as she looked up. ''This device was designed to detonate when it was tampered with. There is—or there was—no actual timer. When we opened the cowling we activated a circuit—look for yourselves.''

Paprovitch picked up the cowling and examined its underside. A tiny magnetic clip stared back at him.

''My God—she is right. We have activated it ourselves!'' His wife sank against him.

Tatiana's voice came again. ''The circuitry is eroding—it appears there is less than fifteen minutes, vastly less I think. And then, it is all gone.''

Paprovitch swept his wife into his arms, kissing her head. ''No!'' He shouted the word into the darkness beyond the lighted laboratory table. And he heard the gunfire outside. It was drawing closer.

## 23

It was evident from the pattern of defense that whatever was being defended lay at the end of a long, narrow corridor. The corridor was like the spoke of a wheel, and at the end was their target, the hub.

Track and Baslovitch had been joined by six of the air police and the base commander. It was the base commander who spoke, through a bullhorn. Baslovitch stood at Dan Track's right ear, simultaneously whispering a translation. "He says, 'Many of you know me, my wife works here. My son goes to school here. The air force major you trusted, the orders he issued to your commanders—all were false. You are protecting a nuclear weapon which will destroy us all, possibly in minutes. So many of us—all of us comrades—have died here tonight. Lay down your arms and we shall lay down ours. It is a time for trust.'"

Baslovitch's voice choked on the last word and Track looked at him. "What is it?"

Baslovitch smiled, the devil-may-care smile Track had become used to.

Baslovitch stepped from cover, his assault rifle over his head. Slowly, he settled it to the floor, his hands empty. He started to walk forward.

Track watched in silence. He swallowed hard, shrugging. "What the hell," he murmured to himself. He stepped from cover, set down the SPAS-12 and then, hands palm outward before him, started after Baslovitch down the corridor.

He looked behind him once. The base commander, his pistol on the floor, walked empty-handed toward the end of the corridor.

Track watched ahead of him now, as men stepped from the cover of doorways, holding their AK-47s as if they weren't quite sure what to do with them. He was reminded of a phrase attributed to Napoleon. A messenger arrived, Napoleon read the dispatch, then exclaimed, "Good God—peace has broken out!" He recognized a KGB officer by the color of his shoulder tabs as the man stepped from a doorway, weaponless. In English, he heard Baslovitch calling, "Anton, you know me. We speak the truth. We can fight and die or find this bomb together and disarm it."

The uniformed KGB man looked down at the floor, then up at Baslovitch. Track stopped and watched. The KGB officer threw up his hands in disgust or surrender, Track wasn't sure which. He muttered a single word, repeating it over and over again, "Da—da," and shrugged. He started toward Baslovitch, arms spread out and the two men embraced.

A corporal ran up to them, breathless, saluted the KGB officer and began to report. Baslovitch translated for Track again. "He tells my friend he has cut the main generator's power supply into the laboratory. They are in total darkness except for emergency lighting over the center of the laboratory, which is sometimes used as a demonstration operating theater. But the door's pneumatic lock is now inoperative and we can't pull it open."

Track nodded, his eyebrows making an arch. He watched the KGB officer as the man barked unintelligible-sounding orders and three men, big men, began working at the door.

The colonel was speaking into a loud hailer and Baslovitch continued to translate for Track. "This is imperative—you must believe us. We will be entering your laboratory in moments. We wish to help you with the bomb. We know all the details, how you have been told it is an American weapon. It is, but brought here by a Nazi. Paprovitch, you are Jewish. Do you wish to serve the Nazi cause? Help us. There is an American with us, a friend, here to help with disarming the bomb.'' Track only wished that he could.

And then an old man came up, a high ranking noncom. He saluted the colonel, said something and the colonel gave him the microphone. Baslovitch murmured, ''A girl in there, a scientist is his eldest daughter.'' He paused, then simultaneously translated as the old noncom spoke. ''Tatiana—this is your father. The truth is that the 500-kiloton weapon will explode any minute, and you will die and so will I and all these good men out here with me and the men and women there with you. You must open this door.''

The man returned the microphone to the colonel. The pneumatic door had opened only a fraction of an inch, the men using bayonets as prybars. But the doors stuck closed.

Track felt sweat running down his face.

Then he heard a voice through the crack on the other side of the door. It was a woman's voice and Baslovitch translated. ''The bomb will detonate in seven minutes. We cannot stop it, papa—but I have released the lock.''

Track waited, tensed, as the men continued to work on the door, prying it open now with comparative ease. He pushed through, running toward the center of the laboratory, the blond-haired young girl suddenly running beside him, saying in poor English, ''Less than seven of minutes now, I think.''

He looked at her, ''How did you know I was American?''

''You all look alike,'' she answered with a straight face.

He reached the center of the laboratory, where a gaunt, bearded man stood looking at him. In good English he said, "This is your work?" gesturing toward the device at the center of the table.

"No more my work than if a terrorist stole one of your country's nuclear devices. Can you stop it?" Track asked.

"No, we cannot," came the firm reply.

Beside him, Baslovitch asked, "Can you delay it?"

"No, we cannot," was all Paprovitch said, as he hugged a dark-haired, rather pretty woman close to his side.

"I can order evacuation—" It was the voice of the air base commander.

"If all cannot be taken to safety, none of us shall leave." It was a white-haired man, his English very British sounding.

"Agreed," the bearded man nodded.

Track turned to Baslovitch. "He has a point."

"Paprovitch?"

"Yeah. The thing did come from my country. If somebody's got to risk a neck it may as well be me." He looked at the air base commander. "Colonel, does the Mi-24 fly much differently than a Sikorsky UH-60 Blackhawk?"

The colonel's eyes flickered to Baslovitch. Baslovitch said in English, "If you know, tell him."

"They are very much the same, Major Track."

Track nodded and pointed to the bomb. "Get some of your guys to get this onto the roof and load her up and get your pilot to preflight it fast and bug out."

"Bug..." began the commander.

"It means leave the cockpit," Baslovitch supplied.

"Point me in the safest direction and I'll fly her out until I've got—" Track continued.

"You will die, my friend," Baslovitch said matter-of-factly.

"No shit," Track grinned. "Get that bomb moving."

Baslovitch nodded, and the base commander barked orders in Russian.

Four men came forward and began to move the weapon, walking as quickly as they could with it.

Track started after them, hearing the base commander saying in English, "Northwest is your only hope, keeping the Ob river to your right, and behind you."

Track broke into a run. The bearded man, Paprovitch, was beside him now. "You must be a minimum of ten miles away from any population center and the blast effect will be minimized if you can get the bomb to the ground before it detonates."

Track only nodded, hearing the girl, Tatiana, saying, "Check your watch—five minutes and forty-five seconds."

"Fucking wonderful, lady," an exasperated Track said, looking down at his watch. At least he wouldn't have time to worry about an afterlife.

He was at the stairwell, his flashlight illuminating it from above as he ran. Baslovitch was somewhere but not in sight. He'd wanted to say good-bye, maybe given the man—the closest to a friend of those around him—a farewell message for George, and for Desiree if she were found alive.

And where was Krieger? he wondered.

Track reached the roof. There was still no sign of Baslovitch as he ran toward the Hind-A and climbed aboard, eyeing the red light flashing from the bomb. He didn't know if it meant anything or not. He looked at the Rolex as he buckled in—less than five minutes. At maximum cruising speed of 229 miles per hour, it could make just a little less than four miles per minute. That made two and one half minutes until he was ten miles from the Academgorodok complex, maybe four minutes before he was at a safe spot to land and then wait it out for detonation. "Shit," he stormed, as he feverishly worked the controls, getting airborne, watching the face of the Rolex. Off to the right he saw a second Hind-A rising from the lawn of the institute. He heard a voice over his headset.

It was Sergei Baslovitch. "I couldn't let a capitalist upstage me—or allow a friend to die alone. I calculate that in less than five minutes the blast will take place. In three we should be safely away from population centers. Give it an extra half minute for security, then a half minute for you to get to the ground, unstrap yourself and run for the chopper. You jump aboard and we are airborne—maybe together we can outrun it, huh?"

"You're nuts—but thanks for thinking of me," Track rasped into his headset. He had the throttle all the way out, the compass heading northwest.

"Such a thing to say to a man who has a one percent chance of saving your life," he heard Baslovitch laugh.

Track felt the muscles of his face tightening as he watched the second hand of the Rolex tick away his life.

JOHANNES KRIEGER OPENED the thin-bladed knife, slowly, carefully. He eyed the blade's target and moved the knife into position again slowly. He touched the blade to the skin, cutting through it, into the substance beneath. The piece of sausage cut now, he folded it neatly in half and ate it, looking at the old woman beside him aboard the passenger car, hearing the click of the rails. He smiled at her, gesturing with the sausage, the woman smiling back. He cut her a piece, feeling in a magnanimous mood.

He handed her the sausage slice, then folded the knife closed after wiping the blade on a rag and placed it back inside his cloth purse and settled the purse on his lap. He replaced the sausage in the basket and closed his eyes, folding his hands over the skirt in his lap.

The woman beside him spoke, and Krieger, in his old-woman's voice, answered that he was on his way to see his son, who was a student at the polytechnic in Moscow. Mentally, he ticked off the time. Finally, unable to stand it any longer, he opened his coat and unfastened the top buttons of his black sweater, lifting the watch pinned to the front of his threadbare white blouse. It showed less than three minutes to detonation, but he would be too far away to see anything except a flash of light in the night.

He let the watch fall to his sagging breast, rebuttoned his sweater and closed his eyes. The old woman spoke again and he opened his eyes to look at her. She was holding out a photograph of her son.

Krieger smiled, opening his purse, fumbling through it and producing a picture of his son—it was actually a picture of Klaus Gurnheim as a young man, before he'd become the master bomber and Krieger's instrument for world domination.

He replaced the photograph in his purse, listening to the woman's idle chatter.

It would be less than two minutes now. And then only one step would remain—the final step, the ultimate act of global terror, at the seat of temporal power.

He chatted with the old woman, waiting for the rumble he might hear in the snowy night. He would express shock and fear. It was part of the characterization.

## 24

Baslovitch's Hind-A was having engine trouble and he had dropped back. Track realized he was going to die. He was less than two minutes out and more than twelve miles from civilization, as he reckoned it. The cruising speed of the Hind-A was faster than Baslovitch had told him.

He started looking for a place to set down, scanning the ground beneath him through the swirling snow to be certain there were no small farms. No village. The earthworms and field mice would have to take to their bomb shelters.

Convinced the area was desolate, he stole a last glance to the Rolex—perhaps a minute and a half remained. He started setting the helicopter down, a humming now growing in intensity from the nuclear device behind him.

There would be no time to release the device from its moorings and take off. No time at all.

He should have left his pistols behind—George would have liked them. He hoped his death wouldn't hurt George's job with the Consortium. He was a good boy, like a son to him.

Desiree—he thought of her, perhaps already dead, perhaps awaiting Krieger's pleasure—and of Krieger getting away with it. Baslovitch was a good man—maybe he would continue to help in the search, or maybe George would get Krieger. Though he'd never told his nephew, he highly regarded the younger man's abilities.

"Desiree," Track whispered into the night, as the helicopter landed.

He watched the second hand sweep nearer to the twelve—one minute.

A voice crackled over the radio. "Run for it—run for it—I'm coming for you!" Baslovitch said.

"No—save yourself!" Track shot back.

"I'm coming—jump aboard—I'll only hover—hurry!" Baslovitch continued.

Track heard him, saw the red light on the bomb. It seemed brighter.

He shrugged and ripped open the seat restraint, jumping through the open door to the snow. He threw himself into a dead run, ticking off the seconds inside his head, seeing the light of Baslovitch's chopper now in the distance, coming fast. "Fifty-five—fifty-four—fifty-three—fifty-two—" He kept running, the Hind-A coming in low and fast, less than a hundred yards from him across the snow. He waved toward it, waving Baslovitch back. There was a high hill ahead of him, and if Baslovitch could get over it would shield him from the blast. With a fast run aboard the gunship he might still survive.

But Baslovitch was still coming. Track threw himself into the run. If Baslovitch wanted to die making a noble gesture, he wouldn't disappoint him. The helicopter was less than twenty-five yards away now, and Track's lungs ached with the cold of the air he gulped, his feet numb in the snow.

The helicopter was skimming toward him, over him. It dipped and Track jumped. The downdraft hammered at him, while the updraft of snow scoured at his exposed face and hands.

Track had a tenuous grip on the stern of the starboard stub wing, near the open sliding doors. His hands slipped where ice had formed on the wing, as the helicopter started to pull up, accelerating. Track's fingers started to cramp, to slip.

He snapped his left leg out, to get a pendulum effect to his body English, then threw both legs toward the open doors, letting go his grip, clawing for the door frame. His legs carried his weight toward the doors, while his right hand skidded along the fuselage skin, his left hand hooking over the door frame.

He could hear, faintly, over the slipstream, "Hang on—I got a radio message from the sergeant's daughter, Tatiana, we have an extra minute—but I didn't tell you so you wouldn't dawdle!" They were skimming the ground, Track's fingers aching, his skin numbed by the icy wind of the slipstream. The helicopter shot over the hill, then down. "Cover your face," he heard Baslovitch yell, "she'll—"

Track lurched his body upward, falling into the helicopter through the open door. A blindingly bright flash assaulted his eyes, and a mammoth roar set his ears ringing as he shielded his face and body. The helicopter rocked and twisted under him from the force of the explosion, almost seeming to stall. The world around him was ripping apart, the helicopter out of control. He looked up. The initial brilliance of the fireball was gone, but the sky was as light as noon. Baslovitch screamed something, and Track saw the Russian holding his hands over his eyes.

Track lurched forward, stumbling into the co-pilot position, grabbing at the controls. He kept low, accelerating to maximum, the sky around him growing brighter in wider and wider diameter, but behind him now as he brought the gunship up to maximum cruise.

"Sergei—answer me—you all right?" Track started.

"I cannot see—the brightness," came Baslovitch's response.

Track looked at the man. He knew little of medicine but the man's face was pinkish red.

"If you get out of this in one piece—if we both do—well, if you need an arm broken on somebody someday, I'm your man," said Track.

The helicopter was at full throttle. They were still alive—perhaps dying of radiation—but still alive. The sky around him and the ground beneath were washed in yellow light and the turbulence was subsiding.

He felt Baslovitch's right hand on his shoulder. "I'll see you again—and we've won."

Track listened to the noise of the slipstream, the noise of the rotors overhead. He could barely hear for the ringing in his ears, but at least he was alive.

JOHANNES KRIEGER HEARD the faint rumble and turned to the window. It would be safe to look for an instant from such a great distance, and he wore dark glasses. He had told his seatmate aboard the train, the old woman, that he had an eye problem. For an instant the sky behind him was as bright as noon.

He smiled.

He had won the day.

One battle remained.

Soon Moscow, and a British embassy worker, a horse-faced blonde who was going home to visit her mother. He could match her appearance identically. His needed items awaited with his allies in the Nazi underground in Moscow.

He would simply murder her, then use her legitimate passport and fly to London, and from there to the United States.

From there to history.

He turned to the old woman beside him, opening his purse, removing the slim-bladed knife, saying to her in his perfect Russian, his voice that of an old woman, "Would you like more of my sausage? It will be a long train ride."

The old woman answered, "I have a loaf of hard bread and an apple. We can share them, perhaps?"

Krieger smiled, turning in his seat, smoothing his clothes over his legs. He began to slice pieces of the sausage as the old woman beside him spread a handkerchief on her lap, like a tablecloth.

The milk of human kindness—it touched him.

# AHERN ON AHERN

I started banging out adventure stories on an old typewriter when I was about ten years old, and I quickly found out that getting published was like trying to hit a home run with a toothpick.

I decided that if publishers wouldn't willingly consider my stories, I'd have to apply some force. The single greatest asset a writer can have is determination. That's something I've always held to be a vital element of a person's life, and something I've tried to put into all the characters in my books.

I was lucky, and was able to combine my love of writing with a lifelong interest in guns. Since 1973 I've written more than five hundred articles on guns, guns and more guns. I still actively free-lance gun articles, test the latest handguns and continue research on the subject.

Hard-won success in the adventure-fiction field didn't come until I was in my thirties with the publication of two series—*They Call Me the Mercenary* and *The Survivalist*. You might say that it only took me twenty-five years to become an "overnight success."

I could not have achieved all that I have without the help of my co-writer, co-conspirator, photographer, lifelong buddy and best friend—my wife Sharon Ahern. Together with Sharon and our two children, Jason and Sammie, I enjoy life on an estate in northeastern Georgia, doing what I like for a living.